Mary Stumpf

At

The Battle of Princeton

Laura Crockett

Woman with a Past Productions

Los Angeles   Trenton

This is a work of fiction. The events, the battles of Trenton and the battle that took place outside of and in Princeton, did take place. These events are a part of the American Revolution and American history. The Stumpf family is a product of the author's imagination.

Mary Stumpf at the Battle of Princeton, Copyright © 2013 by Laura Crockett. All rights reserved. Printed in the United States of America. No part of this book may be used or reproduced in any manner whatsoever without written permission except in the case of brief quotations embodied in critical reviews or articles. For information, contact Laura Crockett, Lauraspeaks@mac.com

www.lauracrockett.com

Cover art by

Victoria Petho

ISBN: 978-0615908779

0615908772

To Jerry

Forever faithful to the Cause.

Contents

Good Reader,

Before you start reading, here are a few things that will help you understand the historical background of the story.

The Stumpfs are Quakers or Friends. This religious organization started in England in the seventeenth century. You will notice that the Stumpfs speak the English language a little differently than the others. The Stumpfs, and most Quakers in this story, speak in Early Modern English. This form of English was spoken in the British Isles (England, Scotland, Orkney, Isle of Man, and Ireland) from 1450 until the modern age, about 1750. It is the language of William Shakespeare.

People who were class conscious spoke Early Modern English. That is why it had a second person, familiar pronoun as well as a second person, formal pronoun. The pronoun **thou** is the second person, familiar, and the pronoun **you** is the second person, formal and plural. How were they used? Anyone who is your friend or an equal to you, would be addressed as "thou." Your parents or betters are "you." If you were speaking to more than one person, the plural, **you** would also be used.

The objective case is **thee**, and the possessive is **thy** or **thine**. So to say to a friend, "You will find it," you would say instead, "**Thou wilt** find it." The verb conjugates as well. All second person, familiar verbs end with a 't.' Below are a few examples. Note that many are spelled with the ending 'st, but it is pronounced like an **est**.

You will/thou wilt
you shall/thou shalt
you would/thou would'st

you are/thou art (past tense of were is *wast* or *wert*)

you do/thou dost

you make/thou makest   or mak'st.

you go/thou go'st

Why did the Quakers use that form of English? Because the Quakers believed in the equality of all people, they addressed no one formally. Therefore, they used the familiar form of the pronouns/verbs *with everyone*. This equality of use made them stand out as a people. Not all, however, used this form of English. You will see that many of the Quakers have picked up the modern usage and dropped the extra pronouns.

The action of the story takes place during the American War for Independence, or as we usually say, the American Revolution. The Crisis period, or the ten crucial days, is at the heart of the story. Those ten days are December 25, 1776, through January 3, 1777. Then, the Americans divided into **Patriots**, those who favored separation from Britain, and the **Loyalists**, those who were loyal to the King. Patriot soldiers were in the Continental Army or the various militias. Loyalist soldiers also formed militias, but British soldiers they referred to as **Regulars**.

Enjoy!

Laura Crockett

The Characters

This book is historical fiction. The characters are both real and imagined. Below is a list detailing the historical and imagined individuals who people this story.

Historical Characters

General George Washington, Commander in-Chief, Continental Army

General Hugh Mercer, Brigadier, mortally wounded at the Battle of Princeton

Richard Stockton, a signer of the Declaration of Independence

Captain William Shippen, Continental Marines

Thomas Clarke, a farmer

Sarah Clarke, a sister to Thomas

Hannah Clarke, a sister to Thomas

Fictional Characters

Mary Stumpf, Samuel Stumpf, Paul Stumpf, children of Jacob and Miriam Stumpf

Jimmy UpDyke, drummer in the Continental Army

Mr. Evans and his children, Suzanna and Edward

Mr. and Mrs. Parker, Loyalists

Lazarus, Uncle Henry, Aunt Dorothea, and other relatives of the Stumpf family

Plus, Mrs. Smyth, A Courier, several Regular Soldiers, the Sniper, Peter and other Americans.

One

Summer of 1775

"Jimmy UpDyke joined the Continental Army!"

"What?" Twelve-year-old Mary Stumpf turned to face her brother Samuel.

"Yes, 'tis true. 'Tis true." Samuel folded his arms and then leaned back against the fence that surrounded the orchard. At fourteen, he had grown nearly as tall as his dad.

"Samuel Stumpf, thou liest!" Mary said it as she marched up to him, wiping the sweat from her face with her apron.

"Oh no, Mary." Samuel looked down his nose at his sister. "He leaves tomorrow. If thou wilt be gentle with me…" his voice trailed off.

"If I will be gentle with thee, what?" Mary stood her ground, looking straight into his gray eyes. She did this because she could always tell when Samuel was teasing by the look in his eyes. He was not teasing.

"Samuel?"

"He'll come to dinner. Today." Samuel looked Mary up and down with a disapproving eye. "That gives thee plenty of time to put thyself into some order."

"But I must pick peaches?" she wailed.

Samuel laughed. Mary's fist clenched, ready to put to his arm.

"Mary?" Mary's mother called from the barn.

"Yes, Mother," Mary replied. She relaxed her fist.

"Bring in peaches for dinner."

"Yes, Mother."

Mrs. Stumpf stepped back into the barn.

"Come." Mary grabbed Samuel by the arm to drag him to the orchard.

"I'll not pick thy peaches for thee," Samuel said, digging his heels into the dirt.

"Then thou wilt not get any for dinner." She did not let go of his arm.

"Ha! Dost thou think Mother will allow it, that thou can'st deny me peaches?"

"'Tis my orchard, Samuel, Mother and Dad have said so. I will tell thee who may have the peaches and who may not. Pick and eat, or stay wanting." Samuel and Mary locked eyes. She was serious.

Samuel rolled up the sleeves of his shirt, and then set to picking. Before long he was as sweaty and disorderly as Mary.

It didn't take the two of them long to finish picking the ripe peaches, after which they placed the filled baskets into the coolness of the cellar. They then turned their attention to the brook by the house. They raced down its steep bank and plunged into the cold water. Instantly, they were relieved from the heat of the day and the sweat and dirt of their labor. After they washed, Mary sat on a rock to keep her feet in the water, while Samuel lay back, allowing the rushing water to run over his body.

"Why does he leave?" Mary asked.

"Who? Oh, Jimmy?" Samuel paused. "Well, it's like this, Mary. He says he is a patriot."

"What does that mean?"

"What does it mean to any of us?" Samuel shrugged. "Ask him. Ask Jimmy."

"Samuel? Mary?" Their dad's voice called to them from the top of the banks. "'Tis almost dinner."

Mary and Samuel reluctantly left their cool oasis to trudge up the bank and into the house. Inside her room, Mary carefully dressed, for she wanted Jimmy to remember her as a pretty girl, not the sweated out, untidy farm girl who picked peaches and weeds on her parents' farm. She paid special attention to her hair, combing it back into a knot that would fit nicely under her cap. When finished, she slowly walked down the stairs. She then helped her mother with the dinner.

Their guest was punctual. The clock in the front room chimed two o'clock as the most perfect Jimmy UpDyke crossed the threshold into the house. His long blond hair was pulled into a tail held in place with a black ribbon. In spite of the heat of the day, he wore his shirt tied up at the throat. His waistcoat was spotless; his breaches were of the whitest linen. His dark blue eyes cast their look over the members of the Stumpf family.

"Mistress Stumpf," Jimmy said with a graceful nod of his head as he removed his hat.

"Come in and sit thee down here," Mrs. Stumpf said, indicating a chair next to Mary's.

After a moment of silence, Mary's elder brother Paul picked up the first dish to serve himself. Mary shoved the vegetables toward Jimmy.

"Won't *you* have some?" Jimmy said, picking up the serving spoon.

"Yes," Mary said in a whisper.

Jimmy served Mary then himself before passing on the dish.

"Jimmy, I understand thou wilt journey to Boston?" Mr. Stumpf said.

"Yes, Mr. Stumpf, so I will."

"When?" Mary asked.

"In the morning I leave with Isaac Chambers."

"Isaac?" Mrs. Stumpf said. "Why, he is of our Meeting here in Stony Brook. That a Friend should fight in this war, I don't care what the Cause—"

"Miriam," Mr. Stumpf cut Mrs. Stumpf off.

"I mean no disrespect, Mistress, but others of your faith have joined the Cause for Independence." Jimmy smiled broadly.

"The Cause being one thing, but the war is something else," Paul said.

Paul, at nineteen, was very grown up. Many times he said things Mary could not understand. As he had at this moment. Samuel would often say that Paul fancied himself a philosopher. What, Mary wondered, was a philosopher? If a philosopher said things one couldn't understand, of what use were they?

"Wilt thou," Mary swallowed hard, "carry a gun?"

4

"No Mary. I'll be a drummer until I turn sixteen. Not for another year." Jimmy smiled at Mary. Mary was relieved to hear it.

Mrs. Stumpf brought out the sliced peaches and a bowl of freshly churned cream. The peaches were praised for their sweetness, which delighted Mary a great deal. The talk then turned to the farm. When the clock chimed 4 o'clock, Jimmy excused himself and left.

Mary felt the agony over his departure deeply. Until that moment, as she watched him walk down the road toward the village, she hadn't known how much she cared for him. She would have run after him if Samuel hadn't stopped her. She paused. In her mind, though, she determined to see him one more time.

That night, as she lay in bed, she couldn't sleep. She kept looking out her window up at the stars. The blinking dots seemed to flash a message to her that held her in a trance. Of course, she thought. In an instant she understood what it was she had to do. Jimmy would have to walk by her house in the morning. Just then, the clock downstairs chimed twelve times. Midnight!

Jimmy would pass this way at dawn, or perhaps even before. If Mary wanted to see Jimmy, she needed to sleep. Her mind was made up. She bounded out of bed and, with a sweep of her arm, grabbed her clothing. Holding her breath, she tiptoed down the stairs. In the front room she dressed. When finished, she took the old comforter from under the great chair and with it, quietly left the house. On the bench under the oak tree that shaded the front yard, she curled up on the comforter. She was soon fast asleep.

Two

Early Morning Farewell

The cold before dawn woke Mary. Already the birds chirped as she opened her eyes to see blackness. It took her a moment to remember where she was and why she was there. She sat up quickly. She listened intently to see if she could hear voices or footsteps. The rooster crowed. Then something buzzed near her ear. A mosquito! She waved it away. She returned to listening for the footsteps. Nothing. She leaned back into the bench. Her arm itched. She scratched it. It was a mosquito bite. She then discovered another one, and then another. Mary sighed. Her overnight outdoor sleeping without a blanket to cover her was the cause of her itchy misery. She scratched.

The voices from the roadway startled Mary into stillness. She listened hard. The voices grew louder as they came nearer. Mary stood up. To the east the light of dawn peeked over the horizon. She walked to the edge of the yard to wait for the bodies that belonged to the voices to pass by. Her eyes, having grown accustomed to the darkness, now made out the forms headed her way. Her breath quickened. She strained to see faces. It was Jimmy's bright blond hair that announced him.

"Jimmy, 'tis thee?" Mary said in a loud whisper.

The figures stopped. She could see the blond hair turn its face to her.

"Go on ahead," Jimmy said to his companion. He then came Mary's way. "Mary? What are you doing here?"

"I came to wish thee God speed."

"Come," he said as he walked to the gate. "Walk with me a little."

He opened the gate for her, moving aside as she stepped out onto the roadway. Side by side they walked, toward Princeton, maintaining an uneasy silence as the horizon opened up to the light of the morning.

"Why, Jimmy, why fight in this war?" Mary asked.

"Ah yes. You would ask that question of me. It's like this, Mary. I have an idea about America, the same idea as many others have."

"Thou wouldst fight for an idea?"

"Yes."

"What is this idea?"

"To be an American citizen. Not a subject of the king. Especially that one."

"George the Third?"

"Yes."

"Thou hast a liking for those men up in Boston and Concord and that other place, those who shot the Regulars?"

"We think alike, Mary, those men and me."

"Thou wilt join with them?"

He didn't answer the question. The morning grew light enough for Mary to see the features on Jimmy's face when he turned toward her.

"I don't like the thought of going into battle. To tell you the truth, Mary, it scares me."

"It scares me, too, Jimmy." She turned away so he wouldn't see the fear in her face. Her throat tightened. She wanted to cry, but she wouldn't allow it.

"This is important to me. This is something a man must do," Jimmy continued.

"Yes?"

"Yes."

They paused in front of the Friend's Meeting on Quakerbridge Road. In her mind, Mary wished it were First Day so that she could be in Meeting. Mary wished she were anywhere but in the middle of this farewell conversation with Jimmy. It was one of those things that she must do, and yet didn't want to do: say goodbye to Jimmy.

"I don't know how you feel about this war, you being a Quaker and such. Or even if you agree."

"War is violence, Jimmy. One man kills another. How can anyone like such a thing?"

"I don't say it's not an awful thing. I say it's a necessary thing; an action a man sometimes has to take. I believe in something, Mary, and that something is bigger than me. It's a fight to be *me*. When someone won't let you be, that's when a body has to fight back. Can you understand that?"

Mary wished she could understand what Jimmy was saying, but at the moment, he sounded philosophical. She sighed as the sun came out and spilled its light over Jimmy's face. He was as beautiful as a flower in full bloom. Mary bit her lower lip. She wanted to reach up with both her arms to draw him close to her. That couldn't be dared. Instead, her arms hung loosely down her sides. Tears welled up in her eyes.

"Ah Mary," Jimmy touched her face. "Don't cry." He peered closely at her features. Slowly, he shook his head from side to side. "You will cry once you see your face."

Mary quickly put her hands up to her cheeks.

"That's right, you have mosquito bites all over your face."

"Oh!"

Jimmy laughed. Mary started to laugh as well, but her chuckles quickly turned to tears.

"I don't want thee to go!" she said, losing all self-control.

For the moment, Jimmy stood without words as he watched Mary's emotional display. After she regained her composure somewhat, he lightly touched her arm. He motioned with his chin that they should walk forward. When they reached that place in the road that went up an incline to the Clarke farms, they paused again.

"I'm meeting Isaac in Frog Hollow."

Mary nodded in response, her face turned down to the ground.

"I confess, Mary, that this excites me, to be off on my own. I shall miss Stony Brook, but the larger world has called my name. Do I make sense to you?"

"Yes," she said. "There are days when I don't want to be on the farm. I don't want to milk a cow or thresh flax. The days I like best..."

"Yes? The days you like best?"

"Are when I take the peaches to market."

"A lady of business." Jimmy smiled broadly at Mary. "I promise you this, I will write. Whenever I can. Isaac tells me couriers are always in the employ of the generals and they will take personal letters as well."

"Yes, yes! Thou shalt write me. Every day."

"I cannot promise that."

"I then shall write thee every day. Thou shalt answer when thou can'st."

Jimmy smiled broadly at Mary again, and she smiled back. Her heart, however, was heavy. She knew the moment of separation was near.

"God speed, Mary. Even though you are a Quaker given to non-violence, please pray for me."

"I will, Jimmy. I will."

He then turned and walked away from her. She stood there in the middle of the road, watching him until he disappeared into the brightness of the rising sun.

Three

Discomfort

All the way home Mary cried. As she neared the front door, it opened for her. On the other side was her mother. Without speaking Mary ran into her arms. Mrs. Stumpf held her daughter close. In those secure arms, the young girl's tears seemed to go on forever. The great sobs hurt her chest; such was her agony. When she had cried herself out somewhat, her mother guided her into the front room. There she directed Mary to sit down on the great chair. From the sleeve of her shift, Mrs. Stumpf pulled out her handkerchief. With its soft linen she wiped her daughter's face. Mary tried to speak, but her throat was sore from her weeping.

"Shush, daughter." Her mother smiled as she spoke. "Thy weeping may cease, but thy sorrow will stay a while."

"Ye-yes."

"Look at thy face, swollen with tears and bites."

"Oh, I know, he-he saw them." Mary threatened to cry again.

"Jimmy? Of course. He is what made these tears come, through no fault of his own."

"Why...why did he have to go away?"

Mrs. Stumpf pulled the small footstool toward the chair. She sat on it so that she could look her daughter straight in the eye.

"He is a young man now, though to me he seems barely a child. Never mind, that is the mother in me who speaks. What I mean to say is that young men must do what they feel is right. His father gives his blessing to Jimmy in this enterprise of war. Therefore, Jimmy has no argument there." She paused to think. "But thou, Mary. Though thou hast feelings for Jimmy, thou art a girl still."

"I don't feel like a girl."

"Daughter, this sadness will lessen over the days. Best for thee is to direct thyself to work." She leaned away from Mary, and studied her face for a moment. "We need bread. Distract thyself there."

Mary nodded her head.

"Now, wash thy face. Cool water will ease the bites as well."

"Yes, Mother."

"Go on."

The two stood up together. Before she left for the kitchen, Mary threw her arms around her mother to hug her close. She felt her pain ease in the comfort of her mother's love. Later, when Mary splashed the cool water across her face, she felt her inner turmoil die down. It was while she kneaded the bread dough that her thoughts returned to Jimmy.

She heard the clock in the front room strike nine in the morning. How far, Mary wondered, had Jimmy gone? When would he arrive in Boston? How, she now realized, were her letters to get to him? In her anxiety of saying goodbye, she had forgotten to ask him just where in Boston he would be. Now she was angry with herself. How could she have been so stupid? Her emotions again threatened to take over, so she applied herself with ever more force to the dough, slapping it, punching it down so hard that she threatened to kill it.

"Who dost thou beat?" It was Samuel.

"Oh, tis thee."

"Yes?" Samuel asked with suspicion in his voice.

"Where will Jimmy UpDyke go?"

"Oh. Is that it?" Samuel's lips moved up into one of his teasing smiles. "Let's see, where did he say he was going? Hmm…"

"Samuel!"

"Demands? Thou hast demands of me?"

"See'st thou this?" Mary pointed to the loaves of formed dough that waited for the oven. "After these loaves are baked, I will make a cake and cobbler. What would'st thou say to that, if I forget to serve *thee* cobbler?"

"If thou would'st pay some attention to what goes on in this world, thou would'st know he goes to Boston."

"I know 'tis Boston, but *where* in Boston? If I write a letter, do I address it to Jimmy UpDyke in Boston?"

"Hmm. What was that he told me?" Samuel made a point of a too thorough search of the pockets of his waistcoat. "Ah, here it is." Samuel had nothing in his hand but a finger that he pointed to his head. "In here."

"Thou art nothing to me but a jackanapes!"

"Now Mary…"

A knock came at the kitchen door. Samuel opened it. Suzanna Evans stood on the other side.

"How are you today, Mary?" Suzanna made a short curtsey, and then made herself at home by sitting on the head chair at the table. She paid no attention to Samuel as he quietly backed out of the kitchen.

"I'm well. And thou?"

"Sad, but such is to be expected when there are partings."

Suzanna was a year older than Mary, but always tried to sound like she was much older. She wore a light blue silk gown that revealed a dark blue petticoat. Around her shoulders she had a white linen scarf that hid the fact that no matter how tight her corset, she, as yet, had very little in the way of a bust line. Fastened around her neck was a light blue ribbon. The sleeve lace matched the lace of her cap. Blue ribbons also held her sunhat fast to her head. Her family's prosperity showed.

"What partings are those?" Mary asked.

"Jimmy UpDyke is gone to Boston. But I suppose you know that?"

Mary returned to arranging her bread dough too neatly in a row. "I have to take these outside," she said, picking up the first two loaves. "Wilt thou open the door for me?"

Suzanna stood up to open the door, and then followed Mary out to the oven.

"You do know that?" Suzanna repeated as Mary shoved the loaves into the oven.

"To Boston, yes."

"Surely you know, Mary, that he is in grave danger?"

"Isn't anyone who goes to war in grave danger?" Mary returned to the kitchen, Suzanna following her.

"Well, of course," Suzanna said.

"Then why dost thou tell me?" Mary, with Suzanna following, returned to the oven.

"Oh," Suzanna paused while Mary placed the loaves in the oven. When Mary turned to face her, she fanned her face. "The day is hot, and it's only ten. How can you stand the oven on such a day?"

Mary shrugged. She returned to the kitchen, Suzanna following. Mary assembled the ingredients for a cake.

"What are you making now?" Suzanna returned to the chair.

"A cake."

"Oh." Suzanna fanned herself. "You will make some farmer a good wife, Mary."

Inwardly, Mary smiled. Jimmy was a farmer's son, and one day, he would be a farmer as well. The thought delighted her. She turned to look at Suzanna. She started to smile, but something about Suzanna's expression troubled her. She went back to mixing the cake. At that moment, she understood that Suzanna was her rival for Jimmy's affections.

"What has happened to your face, Mary?"

"I slept out last night."

"Why would you do that?"

"It was so very hot in my room."

"Are they painful? The bites?"

"No. Itches."

"Don't scratch. It will scar you."

"Mother gave me an ointment for it."

"Your mother is good at these things." Suzanna fanned herself while staring out at the fields across the way. "I heard Jimmy was here yesterday."

"Yes. For dinner." As Mary spoke, she could see Suzanna tighten her jaw. "Samuel invited him. They hunt together."

"I didn't know Friends and Presbyterians kept company." Suzanna rapidly fanned herself.

"Why Suzanna, we are Friend and Presbyterian and we keep, well, some company."

She stopped fanning herself. "We are neighbors. My father buys your Mother's linen cloth to sell in our shop. Oh, which reminds me. I am instructed to inquire if there is more cloth to be had." Suzanna used a high and mighty tone of voice.

"No. She weaves now. Tell thy father next month there will be more linen."

Suzanna stood up as if to go. "Do you," she hesitated. "Do you think Jimmy will write?"

No sooner were the words out of Suzanna's mouth than Mary knew Jimmy had not told Suzanna he would write to her. Mary's heart beat faster. What Mary felt like doing was to be high and mighty over Suzanna, to say to her, "Yes, he promised to write me," but that would be pride. Though she knew she was not to feel pride, at that moment Mary did. That Jimmy had promised to write her and not Suzanna Evans thrilled her. Mary felt the desire to lie to Suzanna, but that too would be a sin. So she thought to answer the question as Suzanna had put it to Mary. Did she think he would write? Then doubt flashed into Mary's mind.

"If he can, he will." Mary looked down to the ground in deep confusion over her own feelings.

Suzanna turned back to look at Mary. "Well, I suppose he will write to me. He knows where I live."

Out came Suzanna's fan again, along with her superiority. She gave a quick curtsey before she left through the kitchen door. Mary watched her through the windows as the haughty girl walked through the yard. When she disappeared around the corner of the house, Mary was relieved.

After dinner, Samuel helped clean up. As Mary washed dishes, he dried them. The two worked in silence.

"Thy cake was awful." Samuel watched Mary's face for a reaction. None came right away.

"My cake?" Mary stopped washing to look up at Samuel. He smiled broadly at her. "What is thy meaning, my cake is awful?"

"Oh, so thou dost hear me," he said, putting the dish up on the rack. "I thought thy mind was in the dirty dish water."

"Meaning?"

"Suzanna stopped me as I came from the village. She questioned me, endlessly, about Jimmy's visit."

"She questioned thee? Thou didst not say anything about this morning?"

"About how those mosquito bites came to be all over thy face?" He looked as if he wanted to laugh, but he held it in. "Little sister, I'll not betray thee."

"I thank thee for that, Samuel."

"It bothers me that thou wouldst even think it." Samuel frowned.

"No, I don't," she pleaded.

Samuel shook his head. He tossed the dishrag onto the table. "I am needed in the fields." Without a further word, he left the kitchen, letting the back door bang shut as he did.

Mary stood motionless at the dish tub, not knowing what to do. She didn't want Samuel angry with her, nor had she meant to hurt him. Jimmy UpDyke caused so much confusion and trouble in her life! She felt tears welling up when she heard thunder in the distance. Mary glanced out the window. A breeze had begun. A thunderstorm was wending its way toward the farm. Mary guessed it would arrive in fifteen minutes, and there were too many ripe peaches on the trees that would be knocked to the ground. She quickly left off the dishes, grabbed the basket by the door, and went out into the orchard to pick her precious fruit.

By the time she finished the second tree, the breeze was stiff. Big, black clouds gathered overhead, promising to dump their contents on the girl atop the ladder picking peaches as quickly as her arms could move. She finished the tree, but there were six more trees to go. Quickly she climbed down, dragged the ladder to the next tree, climbed to the highest branch first, and repeated the speedy motions of picking the fruits. Lightning cracked across the western sky. The basket was filled. She lugged it to the cellar, emptying it as thunder filled the air. By the time Mary returned to the orchard, drops of rain hit the ground. She worked as rapidly as she could, thinking only to save her crop.

As she secured the ladder against the fourth tree, a huge gust of wind knocked it down. She placed it against the other side so that the wind would blow it into the tree, not away from it. Mary climbed it, filling the bucket full of fruit as more lightning brightened the dark afternoon. The thunder was loud. Mary was blown against the tree. The branches and leaves scratched her arms.

Yet she didn't stop. She reached every piece of fruit she could. Then the ladder slipped, shoved forward by a gust of wind. A large branch caught it, stopping its fall to the ground. Another crack of lightning filled the air with such energy that Mary thought she would die. For the first time in her life, she feared for it. She was stuck in the tree, too far up to jump down. She glanced up just as a bolt of lightening streaked across the black clouds.

Now the rain came. Heavy drops hit the ground. She needed help. The ladder slipped forward once more. If Mary tried to climb down it, the ladder would fall with her on it, for the very top rested against the one branch. Another gust hit. Mary could feel the pressure placed on the ladder. She was going to fall. When another streak of lightning cracked overhead, she screamed. She grabbed the branch with both her arms. As thunder shook the tree, with her in it, the ladder fell to the ground.

Four

Strength

The rain came down hard. The wind pushed it against Mary's skirt. She could feel the cloth grow heavy against her legs as it soaked up the water. She struggled to try to balance the weight of her body and drenched clothing. That only made her tired. She then did the only thing she knew how to do. She prayed; for strength and for guidance. Suddenly, it came to her from the small voice inside to stop struggling and stay still. Mary obeyed. The voice continued, telling her to call out. Mary took a deep breath and then, at the top of her lungs, yelled.

"Help!"

She waited. Nothing. No one.

She braved looking down to the ground. Branches were in her way, so she couldn't get a good look. She could see that if she inched her way toward the trunk, she would be able to put her feet on another branch below her. If only, she thought, that second branch wasn't there, directly below, she could drop cleanly to the ground. Or could she? She was near the top of the tree, a good twelve feet up. Mary would have to wait for help.

"Help!" she shouted out again.

Mary then began the arduous task of inching her way toward the trunk of the tree. With her right hand, she was able to grab hold of a smaller offshoot of the large branch. This allowed her to move her left arm down the branch she so desperately clung to. As she moved, the sleeves of her shift tore and her exposed flesh rubbed up against the rough bark of the tree. A stub of a small branch cut her. She grit her teeth. Her muscles grew tired. Finally, she could feel her left foot touch the branch below her. It was then that the sweetest sound in the world reached her ears.

"Mary!" her dad called up to her. His voice was strong, but he did not yell. "Do exactly as I tell thee."

"Yes!" she yelled down.

"Swing forth and then back, and when I tell thee to let go, let go."

"Yes, I hear thee." Mary immediately moved her feet to propel herself forward and then back again. This she did several times, swinging her legs and body up and back. As she did so, she scraped her arms even more.

"Let go!"

She obeyed. She dropped down, missing the larger limb but not completely. The smaller branches and leaves scratched her legs and face. Within seconds, however, she felt two pair of arms catch her. Mary's dad held her body, while Paul took hold of her legs. Paul arranged her in her dad's arms, so that he could carry the bruised girl into the house. There her mother waited; a look a relief on her face. In the kitchen, Samuel poured hot water into a basin. Mr. Stumpf sat Mary on the edge of the kitchen table. He then, along with her mother, examined her many cuts. From her right forearm, her mother removed a small twig that had lodged itself in her skin. Gently she bathed away the blood.

"Hast thou any deep pain?" Her dad felt her legs for breaks.

"No."

"Paul, bring up the tub." Mrs. Stumpf called out.

"A bath?" Paul asked.

"A bath. She is soaked through." Mrs. Stumpf found the blisters forming as she wiped off the caked blood from Mary's hands. She removed her daughter's cap to check her head, but that part of Mary's body remained unscathed except for the many scratches across her face.

Paul brought up the round tub from the cellar while Samuel stoked the fire. They poured water into the deep tub, both cold and hot, until it was nearly filled. Mrs. Stumpf chased out the men, closed the door, and then helped Mary undress. Her skirt, too, was torn. When her mother helped her remove it, leaves fell to the floor.

Mary began to feel the pain of her ordeal, but in her heart she was grateful to her family, and to God. Both had saved her. Both gave her comfort. She threw her arms around her mother.

"We were so worried," she whispered into Mary's ear. "We came in, but there was no Mary anywhere in the house or barn. Paul heard thy scream when he checked the barn for thee. Thy father, nearly at the same time as Paul heard thee, saw thy legs hanging down from the tree." Mrs. Stumpf looked Mary fully in the face. "I have never seen thy father turn white before." She smiled at the memory of it. "Thy peaches are sweet, but they are replaceable. Thou art not. Dost thou get my meaning?"

"Yes. I will never do it again."

After her bath, her mother bandaged Mary's hand and covered her many scratches and bites with ointment.

Mrs. Stumpf gave Mary the next day off. By the end of the week, her bruises and scratches were nearly healed. Even the bites stopped itching so very much. Mary was glad she had nowhere to go. On First Day Mother looked her over. She would have declared the girl fit for Meeting, but she saw the look on her daughter's face.

"Rest up, daughter. Samuel, stay with thy sister."

From the front window, Samuel watched as his parents and older brother walked down the road. When the three had turned the corner, Samuel brought out his guns and set to cleaning them at the kitchen table.

"On First Day?" Mary asked.

"Mary, I am not like thee, to read a book under a tree and call it interesting."

"No, I suppose not."

She watched in silence as he took his long, brown gun apart, cleaning every inch of it until it was shiny.

"No book for thee?" Samuel asked as he polished the brown wood of the gun.

"I have finished the one."

"Thou had'st time all week."

"Samuel, I thank thee for taking my work upon thee."

"'Twas no bother."

They turned silent again. Growing bored with watching him polish his guns, Mary picked up a bit of needlework she had been working on. This she took outside to sit on the bench under the oak tree. After a few moments of embroidery work, she heard the sound of a carriage approaching. There was only the one carriage in the area of Stony Brook, and it belonged to the Parker family who lived in a large house near the village of Maidenhead. Though they lived in Maidenhead, the Parkers liked to attend the Presbyterian Church in Princeton. They were returning home when Mary saw the carriage pass by.

Mr. Parker, a man of forty years, was leaning out the coach window. When he saw Mary seated on the bench, he told his driver to halt.

"You there, girl," Mr. Parker said, exiting the carriage and coming toward Mary.

Mary stood, made a short curtsy, and waited for him to come nearer. She was certainly curious about why he had stopped.

"Is your father here?" Mr. Parker asked.

"No, he is at Meeting."

Mr. Parker fumbled around in his coat pockets for something. "I wanted to ask him if he would come to a meeting Thursday next." Mr. Parker pulled out a small pamphlet from his pocket. "Take this; give it to him."

Mary took the paper and looked down at it. It read, "LOYALISTS! BE NOT SWAYED!" in big letters across the top.

"Do you know his leaning?"

"May I help thee, Mr. Parker?" It was Samuel.

"Oh, yes, I know you. You're the boy who brings our cook fresh game."

"Yes, I do."

"Well, young Stumpf, are you Loyal or do you lean like your friend, UpDyke?"

"This is First Day, Mr. Parker. We do not discuss politics on First Day."

Mr. Parker chuckled at that.

Mary glanced back at the carriage. She could see Suzanna Evans seated inside the coach, speaking to Mrs. Parker, who wore an elaborate hat. Mary was glad she was too far away for them to see the remnant bruisings of her ordeal in the tree.

"Well, these are the times in which we live, young Stumpf, when politics will flood us-or the war will. It's already gone too far." Mr. Parker looked back to the carriage. The women, Mary noted, grew impatient. Mr. Parker turned back to Samuel. "Stay with your family, boy. That's my advice. Don't follow your friend UpDyke. The king takes this colony seriously. He will not lose it. If we cannot come to terms with him, he will overwhelm this bunch of rabble-rousers with his military might. Attend my words. Tell your father to come to our meeting." With that, he abruptly returned to his carriage.

When the Parkers disappeared down the incline in the road, Samuel took the paper from Mary's hands.

"What is this Loyalist?" Mary asked.

"Our sworn enemies."

"*Ours?*"

"They form a militia, to fight for the king."

"Fight? Here?"

"Mr. Stockton says——"

"Mr. Stockton? Thou speak'st to Mr. Stockton of such things?"

"Mary, the entire world speaks of this. Everyone, save thee."

"I have other things on my mind." Mary paused. She looked away into the distance. "I did until Jimmy went away."

"That's what it takes to make thee think about these things?"

"Dost thou hear me talk politics? Really, Samuel, what does this have to do with me?"

"Mary, recall that at one time we drank tea. Now what do we drink in the mornings and afternoons?"

"Coffee."

"Why?"

"Tea is difficult to come by. It's expensive, more so because of…"

"Taxes."

In silence, Mary stared at Samuel. It had been so long since she had had a cup of tea that she could barely remember what it tasted like. She did recall the warm feelings she felt on the winter afternoons when her mother would give them tea and fresh cake with much cream. The coffee was different, thicker, sometimes bitter. She had grown used to it, but it would be lovely to have a cup of tea again.

"I think…"

"Yes, Mary, what dost thou think?"

"I think there is more here than taxes and tea."

"So there is." Samuel glanced up the road. "We must get the dinner laid out, for here come the rest."

Mary glanced in the same direction. Her parents and Paul walked toward the house. She grabbed her needlework from the bench, and then went inside to set the food out. She placed the pamphlet Mr. Parker had given her next to her dad's plate. When he sat, he picked it up and read it over quickly.

"Mr. Parker," Samuel said.

"Of course." Mr. Stumpf wadded up the paper and then threw it across the room into the fire. It puffed into flames quickly. Within seconds, it was ash. There were no Loyalists in the Stumpf house.

Five

The First Letter

Summer gave way to fall. The leaves turned and fell, covering the ground with colors that danced away with the slightest breeze. There would be no more weeds to pull in that garden, no more peaches to pick, until next year. The harvest of the flax was finished. Days now were spent in the sheds turning the long stemmed plant into linen fibers.

Mary hated it. It took hours of beating a plant to strip it of its life so that it could take on a new one. Threshing was tiring in the extreme. Her back hurt, her arms ached. Small pieces of flax waste found their way into her eyes, up her nose, inside her mouth. It seemed to her that she would never rid herself of these tiny, annoying particles. Each night as she dressed for bed, she vigorously shook out each, and every garment, she had been wearing to rid them of the small pieces of raw linen fiber caught in the folds of the clothing. She brushed her hair until it, too, was cleared of specks of plant and dust. Each night when she lay her head on her pillow, she fell fast asleep so complete was her exhaustion. Finally, one morning, when Mary made her way down to the kitchen, her mother gave her the good news that the threshing was over.

"Mary."

"Yes, Mother?"

"'Tis time to start the spinning."

"Yes, Mother."

Her life transferred from the work shed to the spinning room in the upstairs of the house. From daylight to sunset, Mary's days were spent spinning and preparing the thread so that her mother could weave it into cloth. While she spun, she thought of Jimmy. Sometimes she wrote little snippets to Jimmy, pieces saved to include in a letter later. At night, she was too tired to write.

"Mary."

"Yes, Mother."

"'Tis time for thee to take cloth to Mr. Evans."

"Yes, Mother."

At last, Mary could get away from the farm! With her mother's help, she formed the long pieces of linen into rolls, which she then tied with pieces of ribbon. She loaded three rolls and bundles of thread into the back of the little cart. This year, since she was now thirteen, Mary would be allowed to take the precious goods into the village on her own.

Mr. Evans helped Mary unload the cart when she arrived at his shop. Inside, Suzanna was waiting on customers. As Mary entered the shop, she gave Suzanna a short smile and a nod in acknowledgement, which was returned. Suzanna, however, had no smile for Mary.

"Three roles, and six bundles of thread," Mr. Evans said. He took down a ledger book and wrote in it. "Here is your receipt for the items, Mary."

"Thanks to thee, Mr. Evans."

"And, payment for last summer."

Mr. Evans handed Mary a small sack of money. She opened it to look inside, counting it to make sure it was the right amount. "All is correct, Mr. Evans."

"Until next month, Mary." Mr. Evans smiled as he spoke. "I do hope your mother will have more. With this war, goods will become scarce in time. Remind your mother, will you?"

"I will, Mr. Evans."

Mary left the shop to return to her waiting horse and cart. Behind her, she heard the door of the shop open and then close. Thinking nothing of it, Mary climbed into the cart, only to see Suzanna standing to the side of it. Mary was curious as well as upset to see Suzanna there. She sat on the bench and waited for the other girl to speak.

"What do you say, Mary?"

Mary waited, expecting the girl to say more. She searched Suzanna's face.

"Well?" Suzanna said.

"What is thy meaning?"

"We decided," Suzanna stepped forward as she spoke, "to share letters from Jimmy."

Try as she did, Mary could not recall any such conversation or promise.

"We did?"

"Mary Stumpf, you know we did."

"I don't remember the conversation."

"Are you stupid?" Suzanna turned away to return to the shop.

"No."

Suzanna paused at the door, then slowly turned back to glare at Mary.

"How would you know?" With that she opened the shop door to disappear behind it.

Mary stayed motionless. Her mind returned to her recollections of the summer. Mary could not recall anything other than Suzanna's inquiring if Jimmy had promised to write to her. Mary sighed. What difference did it make? He had not written. Not to her, nor to Suzanna, for if he had written to Suzanna, she would have said so. Mary smiled with satisfaction, to know Suzanna had not received a letter.

"Miss Stumpf."

Mary looked up to see the postman, sitting atop his horse, holding a small packet of letters out to her. "If you will take these, it will save me the trouble."

"Oh," was all she managed, taking the letters from his hand. He saluted her before he rode off up the road. Mary turned her attention to the letters. There was one from her aunt in Philadelphia, one from her uncle in Bordentown, and one...what was this? In a large, yet neat hand was a letter addressed to, "Miss Mary Stumpf, Stumpf Farm, Stony Brook, The Jerseys." In the same hand, in small neat letters, near the top, it said, "J. UpDyke, Greene Co., Boston."

Mary's heart skipped. Then she froze. Slowly, without moving her head, she rolled her eyes to the right. There she was, Suzanna, watching her from the window of the shop. Quickly, Mary sat up just enough to shove the letters under her skirt. She picked up the reins, and then slapped them against the horse to make her getaway. In the middle of the road Mary turned around to head to the farm. She did not look back to see that Suzanna had come out of the shop and now stood in the roadway.

"Mary! Mary Stumpf! Come back here!"

A small smile played across Mary's face. She refused to look back.

"Suzanna!" It was Mr. Evan's voice. Mary heard nothing further.

When she arrived home, Mary moved rapidly to unharness the horse. She grabbed the money and the letters, deposited the money in the cash box, hurriedly noted the income in the ledger book, and then gave her mother the two letters addressed to her.

"What hast thou there?" Mrs. Stumpf asked, looking at the letter Mary held in her hand.

"A letter."

"From Lazarus?" Lazarus was Mary's cousin.

"No. From Jimmy."

"UpDyke?"

Mary nodded.

"Well, I shall not keep thee from it."

Mary turned to leave.

"Mary."

She slowly turned to face her mother again. Mrs. Stumpf's face showed concern.

"I know the UpDykes to be of good character. Yet now, at thine age, as thou hast grown much this past year, and womanhood nears, be guarded in thy dealings with young UpDyke."

"Yes, Mother. I will."

"Now go. Read thy letter before thou die'st."

Mary ran up to sit in her room, in spite of the cold, for privacy was what she craved more than the warmth of the fire that burned in the front room. She pulled a chair to the window so that she would have plenty of light. Carefully she opened the letter.

To Mary Stumpf I send greetings from the hills outside of Boston. I arrived here in August of this year, it taking me three weeks journey. Isaac and I traveled on foot and sometimes by wagon, though at the end of the journey we met up with others on their way here, so we were provided with transportation, which made it more pleasant. In September, we were assigned to duties and brigades. The British Regulars keep to Boston where they are well supplied by ships from England. Our arms are limited. I will next travel to Canada.

"Canada?" Mary whispered. She paused for a moment before returning to the letter.

I will write when I return from that journey. Give my greetings to your brothers, Samuel and Paul, and parents. Your servant, James UpDyke.

Mary couldn't help but smile. She refolded the letter and placed it in the top drawer of her chest of drawers. As it was dinner time, she made her way to the kitchen, the smile still across her face. When the family was nearly ready to sit at the table, a knock came at the front door. Mrs. Stumpf went to answer it. At the fireplace, Mary dished the stew into a serving dish. Before she would look up to see her, she heard Suzanna's voice.

"Oh," Suzanna said, "you are about to dine."

"Stay, dine with us," Mrs. Stumpf said cheerfully.

Mary drew in a sharp breath as she placed the tureen with the stew on the table. Suzanna's more frequent visits began to gnaw at her.

"Thank you, Mrs. Stumpf, I will."

Paul took Suzanna's cloak. Samuel pulled a chair out for her. Mary wanted to kick the chair out from under Suzanna. With ceremony, Suzanna sat across from Mary. The family then held their moment of silence before they passed the dishes around. Mary picked at her food. Suzanna ate and talked as if nothing was out of the ordinary.

"Samuel, have you started hunting this season?" Suzanna asked.

"Yes. There are plenty of geese this year down from Canada."

"Canada." Mary said in a somewhat dreamy tone of voice. "Jimmy..." and then Mary stopped herself from speaking further.

"Yes?" Suzanna asked, looking straight at Mary. "You were going to say something of Jimmy?"

"I have bagged three, two sold to the Parkers' cook." Samuel quickly said.

Suzanna paused for a moment, then turned to look back at Samuel. "I hear you supply their very large household. Have you met their son, George?"

"No."

"He studies law at Nassau Hall."

"I have not seen him since he was a boy and would ride with his father along the road," Mrs. Stumpf said.

"They are Loyalists, are they not?" Paul asked.

"So they are." Suzanna smiled.

"And thou?" Samuel asked.

"Samuel," Mr. Stumpf said sternly.

They ate in silence for a few moments.

"The new linen cloth is beautiful, Mrs. Stumpf."

"I thank thee, Suzanna."

The rest of the meal was filled with such chatter. When they had finished, Mrs. Stumpf shoved Mary toward the front room with Suzanna. The two girls were alone, for all the men and Mrs. Stumpf had their jobs to do. The girls sat near the fire as the day was turning colder.

"I saw it. I did."

Mary looked up at Suzanna but held her peace.

"Come, come, Mary. Your silence betrays you."

Mary's stomach pounded.

"What is it thou did'st see?"

Suzanna turned her face away, and stared out the window.

"The letter."

"How?"

"With my eyes, that's how." Suzanna turned back to face Mary. "You want me to believe there's nothing in your heart for him?"

Mary wondered if Suzanna could hear her heart pounding.

"One day, Mary, though perhaps you don't think of such things, we will grow up, and we will require husbands." Suzanna leaned back in her chair, her hands on the armrests. "Jimmy is Presbyterian. And so am I."

Mary hated her for saying it, but she was right. Yet she knew of Quakers married to Presbyterians.

"Mr. Stockton is of my faith, but not Mrs. Stockton."

Suzanna looked down to the ground. "One example does not a habit make."

"Why, Suzanna, do we speak of such things when I am but thirteen and thou art but fifteen?"

"I like to look ahead: to plan my life. There is no harm in it."

"There is a war. Jimmy is in it."

The girls fell silent. The clock chimed. It was four o'clock.

"Jimmy is my friend." Mary said it without emotion.

"I have no quarrel with that." Suzanna now leaned forward, looking Mary straight in the eye. "As long as it remains thus."

"I am amazed at thee, Suzanna."

Suzanna frowned, then quickly smiled. She glanced out the window.

"Oh, look, it grows dark. I must be going."

Mary walked Suzanna to the door. She took the older girl's cloak off the pegs in the foyer and helped Suzanna arrange it around her shoulders. Mary opened the door to a gust of wind that blew leaves into the house. Suzanna turned her face away until the wind subsided. She stepped out onto the front walk, traveling out a few feet before stopping and turning back toward Mary.

"Thank your mother for the lovely dinner." She smiled as she spoke, like a cat does when playing with its prey. She let the smile linger before she continued her walk out of the Stumpf's yard.

Mary slowly closed the door.

That night, as she lay in her bed, she could not sleep. Whether her eyes were closed or open, all Mary could see was that smile Suzanna had displayed with her voice that repeated, "He is Presbyterian, and you are not."

Six

1776

The winter came. Each morning Mary would grab her clothing to run downstairs to dress in front of the fire. Each morning she would take a hand warmer to the barn so the cow would not rebel from the touch of cold fingers while she milked her. It was during these months that baking became the girl's joy. The heat of the oven afforded her a great deal of warmth for the few moments of putting bread dough in the oven, and then later, taking the finished loaves out.

It was during the long nights of winter when she missed Jimmy so very much. He had said he would write when he could, but Mary sighed to think his opportunities were so limited. Perhaps he did write, but the letters were lost.

Winter gave way to spring. The peach orchard was filled with buds! Mary counted the weeks until she had fresh peaches again.

In early June, as she pulled weeds from the kitchen garden, she looked up to see Judge Stockton riding his horse south. He tipped his hat to her, saying, "Good morning, Miss Stumpf."

"Good morning, Mr. Stockton. Art thou for Trenton?"

He stopped his horse. "Beyond. I travel to Philadelphia."

"To the Congress?"

"That is so."

"What shall be done there?"

"Much that concerns us all."

He saw the question in Mary's face. "What dost thou think, Mary Stumpf, of being an American?"

"Not British?"

"Yes."

Mary shrugged. "What would change for me?"

"Ah, thou ask'st what advantage thou would'st gain?" He looked over the fields, then glanced around the farm. He let his eyes wander over the peach orchard. "Thine orchard. Many is the time I have heard talk of Mary Stumpf's orchard and its fruit. Tell me, how would'st thou feel if government restricted thee in the sale of thy peaches?"

"I would not like it."

"Nor does thy father. He cannot sell his flax to France or Flanders or to Holland. He must ask permission to do so."

"I could not sell my peaches to the Dutch? My grandfather is Dutch."

"I think thou take'st my meaning. When we say our liberty, we mean our choice. A free people may choose their friends and their customers. That is what we believe, those of us who want our own nation. No one should make those choices for thee, Mary. Thou choose'st thy friends, thy religion, and to whom thou would'st sell thy peaches. Thou wilt make the choice."

"Yes, I see."

Mr. Stockton's horse pawed the ground.

"A king is like a father, but at some point, fathers bid their children farewell. A good father has no interest in holding his children back." The judge glanced at his pocket watch. "It grows late. I must be off." He turned his horse south. "Give my best to thy family."

"God speed, Mr. Stockton."

He tipped his hat and then rode a way off, but then stopped. He turned back, trotting his horse back to where Mary stood.

"I don't mean to say we will be a perfect nation. But I think our virtues will carry the day."

"Only in heaven is there perfection, Mr. Stockton."

"Right thou art." Mr. Stockton repeated the tip of the hat as he turned his horse away. Mary watched until horse and rider disappeared around the bend.

Two days after that, another letter came for Mary. As with the first, she took it to her room where she sat by the open window. A gentle breeze blew across her face as Mary slowly opened the letter as if it were a precious gift.

To Mary Stumpf, Stumpf Farm, Stony Brook, The Jerseys, does James UpDyke send New York greetings. I received your letter of March this year, from the courier just as we arrived in New York from Boston. The British Regulars left Boston in the spring, and we also left soon after. General Washington says that the British will come to New York because it is key, that we must keep New York. I know nothing of these strategies myself, but do as I am told to do for the sake of the Cause.

I can hear your question, Mary, before you ask it, so I will tell you what our days are like. We are busy preparing, digging up the ground for places to hide, securing the forts, and training recruits. Every day the soldiers train to the beat of my drum. Every day we forage a bit for fresh meat. Many of the officers are frustrated by the lack of supplies. We have run out of blankets, but never mind that for now. The weather is warm enough, though having something soft to sleep on would be helpful.

"My shoes are ruined. My father wrote that he would send me new ones. Some of the men have worn their shoes completely out, so they wrap what is left in rags and keep walking. It is understood that we are still organizing, so the complaints are few. We would like to eat more as well.

"As for me, I am attached still to General Greene's brigade. I have made many new friends among these fellows, which I find agreeable. Though I am forever in the company of others, I miss my family and friends in the Jerseys. Other than that I am in good health and fine spirits. Send greetings to your family and tell Samuel I miss the hunt. Your servant, James UpDyke.

As with the first letter, which Mary had read many times over the months, she folded this one neatly and then placed it in the top drawer on top of the first one. Later, when everyone was asleep she would make her way downstairs to write a reply.

In July the Congress declared independence from Britain. The *Declaration of Independence* was read in several public places. Everyone talked of it. Mr. Parker rode his big black stallion throughout the towns, calling for the Loyalists to declare themselves. As with the Patriots, the Loyalists too made plans and formed into militias.

"You, Mr. Stumpf," Mr. Parker said as the Stumpfs worked their cornfields. "What is your stand on this? Patriot or Loyalist?"

"Mr. Parker, leave off this talk."

Mary tried not to look at Mr. Parker as he spoke. She kept to her weeding, though she allowed her ears free range. Samuel stopped his work to eye Parker as he sat on his large horse leaning over to speak to their father.

"We must all declare ourselves, one way or the other," Mr. Parker said.

"No, we mustn't. There are those of us who keep to ourselves."

"No man can keep to himself. You may think you can, to keep your head in your field while politics goes on around you." Mr. Parker then leaned down close to Mr. Stumpf's face. "Politics, sir, has a way of finding a man whether he likes it or not."

"Get thee off my field, Parker."

Parker paused, seeming surprised that Farmer Stumpf would order him away.

"Don't play the fool with me, Stumpf." Mr. Parker looked out over the Stumpf fields, the corn next to the flax and the flax across from a field of wheat. "You are prosperous, Farmer Stumpf. It would be an awful thing if anything were to happen."

"Is that a threat?" Samuel spoke with anger in his voice.

Mr. Parker started to say something, but glancing quickly at Samuel's father, he thought better of it. He turned his horse away. "Think on it, Mr. Stumpf. The king is in a forgiving mood."

"The king is no friend to us!" Samuel shouted out.

Mary stopped her work to stare at Samuel. She had never seen him in such a state. Mr. Stumpf pushed Samuel back behind him. Mr. Parker looked sternly at them both.

"That one," Mr. Parker said, pointing at Samuel with his riding crop, "has fire." He then abruptly turned his horse around. He looked directly at Mr. Stumpf. "It pleases me to see someone has the passion." With that, Mr. Parker urged his horse right into a gallop.

When he was certain Mr. Parker was out of earshot, Mr. Stumpf turned toward Samuel. "Thou shouldst mind thy tongue."

"I can't stand the man."

"Then sell him no game come the fall."

"I will not."

"It will cost thee. This independence will cost us all."

"I'll sell to the army."

"The army?"

"'Tis well known they're in need of food."

"The army is in New York. How wilt thou get the game to New York?"

"They will come here, I think."

Mr. Stumpf paused to think. Then he said, "Perhaps." He returned to his work and Mary with him.

Samuel stood still, his eyes staring off into a distance Mary could not fathom.

The summer wore on with neighbors talking and arguing all through the village. Even after Meetings on First Day there could be great differences of opinion on this idea of a United States of America. The talk became even more intense in August, when the thousands of British and Hessian troops landed on Staten Island.

"There are thousands of Hessians," Mr. Evans said to Mary when she came into the shop to make a delivery.

"Hessians?" Mary asked. "Who are they?"

"Soldiers from Hesse, a German principality."

"What have they to do with us?"

"Nothing, except the king has hired them to supplement his own army."

"Hired? Thou mean'st to say they are paid to come and fight here?"

"They are." Mr. Evans opened his cash box to take out a small pouch of coins. "Your payment from the spring."

"I thank thee, Mr. Evans."

The idea of foreign soldiers bothered Mary. Not for herself was she frightened, but Jimmy was in New York. It would be Jimmy who would have to deal with these men from Germany. As she walked down the street to the next place she must visit, she heard the talk around her. There were those who liked the idea of the United States, and there were those who thought it mad. Mary sold a large basket of peaches to the man who owned the mill. She smiled at him when he handed her the money. Her money. It was then that Mary recalled what Judge Stockton had said to her.

"Sir," she said to the owner of the mill. "What dost thou think of this conflict?"

"Of our war for independence? Can't say as I like war, Mary, but I like what we aim for."

"To be free to make our choices?"

"I see thou hast spoken with Mr. Stockton."

Mary nodded her head.

"Well, I am for it."

"Then when thou shalt be in want of more peaches, I will sell them to thee."

"Ah, thou art a Patriot, eh Mary? Let not *any* man tell thee it will be easy."

"No sir, for I am well aware of that."

The owner smiled at her as he took the basket into the mill. Mary made her way back to her cart. Later, she said nothing to Samuel or Paul about her decision to be a Patriot. Just how she should support the Cause she could not tell anyone if they asked. She felt, deep within her, that she would be called to participate, but that would be later. For now, summer turned into fall and life, for the Stumpfs, remained routine.

In mid-November Mary received another letter from Jimmy.

To Mary Stumpf, Stumpf Farm, Stony Brook, The Jerseys, does James UpDyke send New York greetings. I must hurry for the last courier will soon leave. We are losing New York. I do not know what will become of us, but there is talk of leaving here. All seems lost. More later. James UpDyke.

"Samuel!" Mary called out as she ran down the stairs. Samuel sat in the front room with a broadside pamphlet in his hands. Mary held out the letter.

"He says New York is lost."

"Jimmy? So I've heard." He held up the broadside that described all that had happened in New York.

"What will happen to Jimmy?"

"What happens to him is what will happen to the army."

"That is what?"

Samuel looked away.

"What Samuel? Tell me."

"He sent that letter when?"

"Two weeks back."

"The army already left New York." Samuel glanced down at the broadside. "The Stocktons are packing up to leave Princeton, along with half the town."

"Why?"

"The Americans will come this way. Following them, to capture them, to end our war, will be the British." Samuel held the broadside out to Mary. "It's from Parker. They call for the arrest of all who signed the Declaration. Mr. Stockton affixed his signature to the Declaration. He is a wanted man, Mary. It will not go well for him if he's captured. Parker means to see him taken."

Mary sat down in the great chair. She didn't take the broadside. "What does it say?"

"That the king will forgive us if we sign a loyalty oath."

Mary and Samuel sat silently, each with his own thoughts. The fire snapped, and the clock ticked the seconds, while for the first time in their lives, the sister and her brother feared for their future.

During the next weeks, their neighbors and fellow Friends talked of nothing else except the war being lost. Many Patriots were distressed at the news. The Loyalists were happy. There were others who did not care which side won. They only wished to go on with their lives as before.

For them, ending the fighting and disruption it brought would be a good thing.

"Over?" Mr. Evans said when he came to the Stumpf house to bring Mrs. Stumpf her money for the sold cloth. "No, Mrs. Stumpf. It is my opinion, and the opinion of others, that Divine Providence will prevail. That at this moment, as General Washington leads half his army across the Jerseys, he will regroup in Pennsylvania."

"Pennsylvania? Why, they may travel through here, then," Mrs. Stumpf said.

"Most likely they will, Mrs. Stumpf."

"Could they do battle *here?*"

"It may come to that."

"Surely, no…"

"I am prepared for that eventuality, mistress. So too should you."

The talk of armies coming marching through New Jersey, and people fleeing their homes, frightened Mary. Yet, she was curious about it. Besides, there was also the thought that Jimmy might march through Princeton along with Washington and his men. In two days time Mary heard that the Americans had arrived in New Brunswick, which was only a day's march from Princeton. Later that night, when all had gone to bed, Mary quietly slipped out of her room, to Samuel's across the hall. She knocked lightly on his door. At first, he did not answer. Mary lifted her hand to knock again, when the door opened.

Samuel whispered, "I thought it might be thee." He stepped back, allowing her to enter. He took her arm, directing her to sit on his bed. Taking the comforter, he placed it over their heads so that their voices would be muffled.

"When will they get here?" Mary whispered.

"Who? The army?"

Mary gave Samuel a dirty look.

"In the morning."

"To march where?" Mary asked.

"To the ferries, to go across the river."

"How dost thou know that?"

"Mr. Evans. He says someone has commandeered all the boats along the river. He thinks Washington will cross over."

Mary kept silent. She sighed.

"By which road will the army come through?"

"The King's Highway."

"Wilt thou go with me?"

"Dost thou think to see Jimmy?"

"Why else would I want to see the army?"

"They will come through early. Be dressed by six."

Mary nodded. As silently as she had come to Samuel's room, she left it.

Before dawn the next morning, she woke up with a start when the rooster crowed. Without a sound, in the darkness of her room, she gathered up her clothing in her arms. Just as silently she made her way downstairs. In the front room, Samuel sat by the fire, which he had stoked up to a bright frenzy. The clock on the mantel told the hour. It was five minutes before six. In the kitchen, that fire too had been stoked to a blaze by Samuel. At that moment Mary loved her brother very much indeed for the kindness and understanding he showed her. By the light of the fire, Mary dressed with haste, yet took time to smooth her hair under her cap and press smooth her skirt. If she did see Jimmy, she wanted to look her best for him.

Samuel waited for her at the front door. He wore his coat and had Mary's cloak in his arms. Without speaking they began their journey, their breath curling in front of them like graceful dancers as they made their way toward the village. When they reached Stony Brook, Mary and Samuel were not alone in the quest to see the army pass by. Many waited, lined up along the Mill Bridge that crossed the brook. Samuel helped Mary to stand on the rock wall that served as a barrier on either side of the bridge. From that position, they had a vantage point.

She heard soft talk scattered among the populace. Someone pulled out a pocket watch to announce the time as 7:05. Mary turned toward the east. The first of the sun's rays were inching over the horizon. She welcomed it, hoping it would bring some warmth to the frigid morning air.

"Well, if it isn't the king's man himself," the townsman named Tom said.

Mary turned back to the road to see Mr. Parker seated on his horse, waiting at the southern end of the bridge.

"He's here to gloat," Tom's wife said.

"Let him have his moment of glory, for he won't have another."

"Don't you be boastful, Tom. He has more reason then we do to feel superior."

Mr. Parker stayed put. Then, a murmur started from the northern end of the crowd of people gathered. Mary turned to see the army coming her way. Leading the troops was a most elegant man riding a dark horse. His boots were polished. His cloak was parted enough to reveal tan breeches. His hat was worn so that she could see his face. His nose was straight, but he was still too far for her to tell the color of his eyes. Mary thought the man was deep in thought as he looked straight ahead without any emotion. Next to him, also riding a dark horse was a black man. On the other side were two other riders also in cloaks.

"Who is he?" Mary asked Samuel.

"Must be Washington."

"Yes, tis he," Tom said.

Mary stood on tiptoe, straining to see beyond the men on horses. It took so very long, so she thought, for the general to reach the bridge. Now, beyond them, she could see the hundreds of men who trudged along in their escape of the British who followed perhaps a day or two behind them.

As the marching army crossed the bridge, Mary noticed that many soldiers had no winter coats, some had no shoes, and all of them looked tired. Mary's eyes danced from face to face, looking for Jimmy. More soldiers came onto the bridge, it seemed they would go on forever, and yet she would not have them end until she saw Jimmy. When the last man crossed, and she could see there were no more to come, Mary's disappointment was keen. Samuel, too, had been looking for the blond-haired Jimmy. He, too, looked disappointed.

On the way home, they walked in silence. Though she felt like crying, Mary held in her tears. From behind them, they heard a horse's hooves approaching. They stepped to the side of the road to see Mr. Parker astride his big horse.

"What a glorious army," he said as he laughed at Samuel and Mary.

Mary, who had a hold of Samuel's arm, felt him tighten. "No, Samuel," she whispered.

"Come along with me to Princeton to meet General Cornwallis, that's Lord Cornwallis to you, you bunch of ragged rebels. He is a real general." Mr. Parker stopped his horse. "Most of your army is taken prisoner, or dead!" Mr. Parker then galloped off up the road, his laughter trailing behind him.

"Jimmy…"

"No, Mary, think'st not that."

"What do they do with the prisoners?" Mary asked.

"I don't know."

"It's bad," Mary said. "Listening to all the talk at the bridge, why, they say this war has ended."

"It's not over." Samuel said it with an intensity that frightened Mary. "Dost thou hear me, Mary? It's not over!" Realizing his overwrought feelings, Samuel paused to regain his balance. "Jimmy will come back," he whispered to her.

Samuel had tears in his eyes. It was the first time in her life that Mary had seen him cry. She took his hand as the morning sun spilled across their faces. It was warm and bright, yet their hearts were dark and heavy as they walked up the road toward home.

Seven

Soldiers

At the sound of many horse hooves coming from the road in front, Samuel peeked out the window. "There's more."

"More of what?" his father asked.

"Soldiers."

"Get away from the window."

Though he seemed reluctant to do so, Samuel obeyed. He took his place next to Paul who sat on the floor soaping the harness to keep it supple. Mary sat by the fire, writing in the ledger book, making a list of items they would need for the spring planting. Her father watched over her, correcting any mistakes she made. Upstairs, their mother tended to her weaving while the light was good.

A shot rang out.

Mary's pencil froze in mid-air. Mr. Stumpf pushed her down to the floor next to Paul. Her heart raced. Samuel jumped up. Standing to the side of the window, he peeked out.

"Stay," Mr. Stumpf said to Mary. He then took a place at the other window. Soon they heard horses racing back toward the house.

"They're headed toward the brook," Samuel whispered loudly.

"Who?" Mary whispered back.

"British Regular soldiers."

"Who fired the shot?" Mary asked

"I don't know."

The horses stopped. Mary could not stand it a bit longer. Without notice, she crawled out of the room to the back bedroom, opening, and then closing the door as silently as she could. She stood to peek out the window. On the road in front, four soldiers in the red-coated uniforms worn by British Regulars sat on horses. There were two more horses that were riderless. After a moment, two soldiers on foot walked up from the brook. They spoke to the others, pointed toward the trees and then to the brook. After a minute, they remounted their horses. The two who had been down at the brook rode toward the village, while the other four trotted off in the opposite direction. Quietly, Mary slipped back into the front room to take her place next to Paul.

"Thou hast no discipline, Mary," Paul said.

"Didst thou notice I was gone, or wast thou too busy staring out the window?"

Paul blushed.

"That seems the end of it," Mr. Stumpf said. The clock struck twelve.

"I'll get the dinner ready," Mary said as she marched into the kitchen. She stirred the soup that had been cooking in the pot, took out bread and cheese, and lay all on the table. She noticed there was no butter. She would have to retrieve some from the icy cellar.

In the cellar, while she cut off a chunk of butter, she heard footsteps. She looked toward the stairs, thinking someone was coming down them. No one came. Her eyes wandered to the small window above, near the ground level of the cellar. There she saw the legs of a man crouched against the glass. Someone was hiding. She gasped but did not call out or scream. With a racing heart, she walked to the window. The boots did not belong to a soldier. She angled herself against the wall for a better view. Here she could see the man wore civilian clothing, like a woodsman. His face, covered with a wide brimmed hat of leather, was turned toward the orchard. After a moment, he turned down to look at Mary. Her heart beat even faster. He brought his index finger up to his mouth. Instinct now told her someone else was out there as well. After a moment, without making a sound, the man quickly left.

Mary ran up the steps, placed the butter on the table, and then quietly slipped out the back door. When she came to the oven, she stopped to peek around its dome. She saw no one. With light steps, she ran through the orchard, keeping to the fence along the banks of the brook. When she came to the place where she was able to see down into the brook, she was shocked to see the body of a British soldier lying face down in the water. She backed away. She glanced all around to see if anyone saw her. Lickety-split, she ran back to the kitchen door. Just as she reached for the knob the door opened. Her mother reached out and grabbed the girl, roughly drawing her inside.

"Get thee in here and be quick." Mrs. Stumpf shut the door quickly. "What dost thou think to be out in this?"

"In, in what?"

"Play not the fool with me!" Mrs. Stumpf kept hold of Mary's arm as she led her to the cellar. At the bottom of the steps she turned to face her daughter. "I saw thee, and saw him as well."

"Thou saw'st the soldier?"

"And the man who killed him." Her mother stopped to think. "Say nothing to thy father of this. If the Regulars return, they will question us. 'Tis best the men know nothing."

"Yes, Mother, but——"

"He did it with a knife." Mrs. Stumpf was visibly shaken. "I have never seen a man murdered…"

"'Tis war, Mother."

"War on our doorsteps." Mrs. Stumpf made her way to the cabinet where rum was kept. She opened a small cask, poured a bit into a saucer nearby, and sipped it. "Whenever there are soldiers about, I don't care which side, thou art to stay inside this house. Understood?"

Mary nodded. Mrs. Stumpf then pointed to the steps. "Go."

Mary obeyed. When she reached the kitchen, she called out to the men to come to dinner. Mrs. Stumpf then came up from the cellar, her face much more composed.

"Didst thou see the soldiers, Mother?" Samuel said.

"Was that the ruckus I heard?"

"Hast thou no curiosity, Miriam?" Mr. Stumpf asked.

"Jacob, I must take advantage of the light. I've no time to gaze out the window."

Mary had never heard her mother lie. The war, it seemed, made people behave in ways they would normally not.

"I wonder what happened down there," Samuel said.

"What didst thou see?" Mrs. Stumpf asked matter-of-factly.

"Nothing. Soldiers looking for someone."

"And found no one. Eat."

Mary looked her mother fully in the face. "When wilt thou have a new bolt for Mr. Evans?"

"Tomorrow. Though perhaps with soldiers riding freely on the roads, Samuel shall go with thee to the shop."

Mary nodded. Suddenly she thought of the British soldiers and how they would look for the man she had seen. She quickly ate her meal, thinking only about the man and how he would have left footprints in the mud.

"I've left something in the barn," Mary said rising and exiting out the door. Once outside she went immediately toward the barn, noting the footprints on the ground, leading from the barn to the house, and then on to the orchard. Inside the barn she picked up the rake, and then with its use, she destroyed the footprints. At one point, she looked to the kitchen window. Her mother stood watching, but when seen, she quickly turned away and left the window. As any good Patriot would do, Mary continued her job until she could not see a boot print anywhere of the fighting Patriot who would forever be nameless.

After chores the next morning, Samuel and Mary took their mother's linen bolt and several skeins of thread to Mr. Evan's shop in Stony Brook.

"Good morning, Mary," Mr. Evans said as they entered his shop. "Have you heard the news?"

"What news?"

"Humph." This came from Suzanna who sat on a stool in the corner.

Mr. Evans lowered his voice. "A Regular was killed yesterday, somewhere upstream. He floated all the way down to the mill paddles before anyone noticed him."

Samuel started to say something but Mary stopped him. "The banks are steep, Mr. Evans. 'Tis hard to see unless one looks straight down."

"You're right, Mary. It's easier to see things from the bridge. Suzanna, log in this bolt and thread." Mr. Evans stepped to the window. "The soldiers were up and down this road several times yesterday. I am certain we shall see them today as well, though with questions on their lips. It has caused excitement, which adds to the foreboding so many feel."

"The war is not over, Mr. Evans," Samuel said.

"It *is* over. If Washington attempts to return, he will only be destroyed by the Regulars and Hessians posted all along the river." Mr. Evans tucked the bolt of linen away. "They arrest us, did you know that young Samuel?"

"Yes."

"Dozens of our neighbors are imprisoned in Nassau Hall," Suzanna said with a great deal of importance. She smiled at Samuel.

"Mr. Stockton was arrested," Mr. Evans said.

"What?" Mary couldn't believe that such a man as the judge should be taken.

"Oh yes, taken by that Parker and turned over to the British. All of us need to watch ourselves. Best you two return home, before the soldiers start questioning everyone on the roads."

Once home Mary let Samuel tell the story of what they had heard from Mr. Evans. Mrs. Stumpf let out a sigh of relief that her men knew nothing so if the British soldiers came by, they could answer honestly. Mary wondered, though, what she would say if the British Regulars questioned her. It did not take long for her to find out, for that very afternoon, soldiers knocked on their door. Mr. Stumpf answered it.

"Good afternoon, Mr...." the British soldier asked.

"Stumpf."

"Are you the owner, or hired hand?"

"This is my farm."

"Lieutenant Cubberson at your service." He touched the edge of his hat. "Have you seen any rebels on your lands, your fields, or any place along this road?"

"Have seen only thee and thy men. Why dost thou ask it?"

"One of my men was murdered, Mr. Stumpf."

"We heard of it."

"But saw nothing?"

"Have I not said just that?"

The solider looked into the house to see Mary standing behind her dad, listening.

"And you, miss, what have you seen?"

"When the soldiers patrol I am not allowed out."

"I see." He looked beyond to see Samuel, too, listened to the talk at the door. "You, what did you see?"

Samuel shrugged. "From the window, the same as my father."

The soldier took in a deep breath. "I will search your barn and yard." He touched the edge of his hat again as he walked away. He made his way around the outside of the house, walking slowly, searching the ground for clues. Mary guessed he looked for footprints. She prayed that her raking the night before was thorough and that all the extra boot prints would be gone.

When Lt. Cubberson turned the corner to walk to the backyard, Mary crossed into the kitchen to watch him from the back window. He made his way to the barn, inside it, then back out, keeping his attention to the ground. At one point he knelt down to examine one of Paul's clog prints in the mud. The prints led to the forge. Lt. Cubberson then continued his search. He crossed the yard, made his way to the orchard. He walked along the fence. He then came upon the point where he could view the brook. Mary could see it startled him. He sharply turned to look at the windows of the house. He worked his way to the kitchen door. Mary stepped away from the window. He knocked on the door. She opened it.

"You can see the brook from your orchard."

"Yes."

"Yet you say you saw nothing?"

"What is thy meaning to question a girl so harshly?" Mr. Stumpf asked from across the room.

"Any of you may have seen this murder take place. My men recall stopping here yesterday to search for a rebel who makes trouble for us." The soldier now stepped into the house. "From the second floor windows the brook can be observed as well, and yet no one saw anything?"

"We were downstairs, in the front room."

"All of you?"

Mr. Stumpf did not answer. Mary knew why. It was like an admission of guilt, so she cleared her throat as if to say something, but she was too late. The officer walked rapidly across the kitchen, found the stairs, and made his way up. Mr. Stumpf followed with Samuel and Mary at his heels. He opened the door to Mary's room. Mary knew that, from that room, he could see only the bend in the brook's bank and the road in front. He stepped over to the weaving room. He opened its door to see Mrs. Stumpf busily weaving. She finished her row and then slowly turned to see Lt. Cubberson standing still looking at her.

"Yes?" she said.

"Excuse, madam," he said as he walked across the room. He looked down to see the brook. He turned to Mrs. Stumpf who sat quietly watching him. "I see the brook is in plain view."

"So it is."

"What did you see?"

"See?" Mrs. Stumpf turned to face her loom. "This. This is what I see, every day, from Monday morning to Saturday afternoon."

"You say, madam," he walked toward her, "you have this vantage point and yet you see nothing?"

"To see something, one must look at it."

"Perhaps I should rephrase my question. Did you hear anything?"

"Horses, someone fired a gun, but then thou art a soldier and soldiers fire guns. The men were speaking, then more horses, and then nothing."

"And this did not make you curious in any way?"

"I had work to do. I have work to do now." She looked the soldier in the eye.

There was complete silence.

"Mother?" Mary swallowed hard. "Shall I make coffee for the soldier and offer him cakes?"

Mrs. Stumpf took her eyes off the soldier and looked to Mary. Lt. Cubberson turned his body toward her.

"Why—" Mrs. Stumpf began.

"Thank you kindly, but my men wait. I must be going."

He marched out of the room, Mr. Stumpf following. Mary ran to her mother. They held each other close. They listened. The door downstairs opened and closed. Mrs. Stumpf took in a deep breath and let it out.

"Thou didst well, Mary."

"Mother, did'st thou lie?"

"Well, let us say that I told not the whole truth."

"And me?"

"Thou?" She shook her head. "In such times we can be confused by what we must do. What others must do." She sighed. "I don't like war, but worse is the thought that we could be arrested and sent to Nassau Hall, there to be imprisoned with many others."

"Mother, art thou a Patriot?"

"I am a practical woman, Mary. Though I suppose I could be called Patriot. Such a thing, as being a Patriot, Mary, comes with an awful price."

"A price?"

"There may be more times when we will be called upon to skirt the truth, for the lives of others may depend on us doing so."

In her heart, Mary understood her mother. Yet unlike her, Mary enjoyed the thrill of the times in which they lived. The day-by-day life of the farm interrupted with soldiers and Patriots, plus the death of the soldier in the brook, had given Mary an entirely new view of life. For the dangers of the world had come to the the Stumpf farm and with it, a heightened sense of life.

"Now be off. I still have some light left."

Mrs. Stumpf returned to her weaving. Mary glanced out the window for only a moment. There, in a tree across the brook, sat the Patriot. Mary could have sworn the man winked at her.

Eight

Christmas

Christmas Day dawned crisp and bright. Mary made bread.

On the spit in the kitchen, a new ham was roasting. Mrs. Stumpf smoothed a new linen cloth across their table. Extra chairs were brought in for that day they would have guests for dinner.

"It's clouding up. It will rain soon," said Samuel as he entered with the geese and ducks he had shot that morning.

Outside, by the oven, Mary pulled the bench up closer to take advantage of its warmth. Even though a light rain now fell, she wanted to stay outside. She heard the guests arrive, and soon her friend Rebecca joined her by the oven.

"The British have put Judge Stockton in prison," Mary said.

"So I've heard," Rebecca said.

"Where is he, I wonder?"

"I was told New York."

"Why all the way there? Why not here, in Nassau Hall, like everyone else they've arrested."

Paul came out to join them. He didn't sit on the bench, but stayed standing by the oven. He smiled sweetly at Rebecca. She blushed and then quickly turned back to Mary.

"Did I hear Mr. Stockton mentioned?" Paul asked.

The young women nodded in unison.

"Many Americans are held on prison ships, though Stockton being a judge, perhaps he is held elsewhere."

"He is called a traitor, Paul." Rebecca quickly looked up to Paul, and then just as quickly looked down to the ground.

"So he is. Under British rule and law, he is a traitor."

"What other law is there?" Rebecca asked.

"Well, none as we are rebels and the Congress has made no new laws except concerning the army and some commerce, and, well…"

"Well what?" Mary asked

"Would'st thou like to see the new calf?" Paul asked Rebecca.

"Oh, yes," Rebecca said as she bounded up in one motion.

So, that was the way of it, just as Mary suspected, that Paul was very sweet on Rebecca. He would ask to court her soon, or so Mary guessed. Thoughts of her brother's romance led her to thoughts of Jimmy. She had not heard from him for over a month. Like many others in the Jerseys, her heart was troubled. Not only over the narrow escape taken by the Continental Army, that alone was not what worried her. It was that feeling she felt in the pit of her stomach over Jimmy. Something awful had happened to him. She was certain of it. Even the lighthearted talk during the dinner could not take away the nagging dread Mary felt. Where, she wondered, was he on this day? Was he well fed? Warm? She had heard so many rumors about the treatment of the Americans by the British that she feared he was hungry and cold.

As it grew dark, the guests were anxious to get home, for the rain's intensity increased. Before Mary finished her evening chores the rain turned to sleet and a wind was picking up. She was happy to return to the house and curl up in front of the fire in the front room. Her mother read to them, from the Bible, the passage about the birth of the Christ child. When she had finished, they said their good nights and then made their way up to their beds.

The wind rattled Mary's windows. The sleet turned to snow. She undressed as fast as she could so that she could sink down deep under the covers. As the bed warmed around her body, she listened to the music made by the wind whipping against the trees. To this tune, Mary fell asleep.

During the night she dreamed of Jimmy. She saw him in battle, beating his drum, soldiers lined up behind him. He stood on a hill facing the enemy. With his *ratatatat* drumming, the troops followed him down into the midst of the enemy. Guns fired, yet they were silent. Men ran but there was no sound of footsteps. All was chaotic as they ran every which way. Still Jimmy played, smiling all the while, *ratatatat, ratatatat, ratatatat.* That was the only sound Mary heard. Jimmy then turned slowly away. In the dream, Mary saw her arm reach out to him. She nearly touched him, but he continued to turn away. When his back was to her, she reached out again. She was so very desperate to touch him.

Ratatatat, the drum played while Jimmy walked away. *Ratatatat,* soldiers came in between them. Her feet mired in the mud, Mary struggled to move. She opened her mouth to call out his name, but no sound came. She tried once more, mouthing the word "Jimmy." Instead, she heard a faint sound like thunder. She turned toward the sound. It repeated.

Mary woke up with a start. She really did hear something like thunder. How could that be? Out of the fog of a heavy sleep, she forced her eyes open. Her room had that bright hue that meant it was snowing.

Kaboom. The sound was distant, but it was there. Something was happening. *Kaboom, kaboom.* The stillness of the morning seemed to funnel the sound to her. She went to the window. The world was white and growing thick with a heavy snowfall. *Kaboom.* She strained to see something, but she could only see flakes falling rapidly down from the clouds. She grabbed her clothing and dashed downstairs. Samuel stood at the front window. He too had heard it.

"Get dressed," he said to Mary without turning her way.

In the kitchen, the fire had been stoked and burned brightly. Mary shut the door and dressed quickly. She did not look presentable, but her big cloak would cover her many faults. Quietly, with Samuel, they left the house.

Outside the *kabooms* were a bit louder.

"It's coming from the south."

"Trenton?" It was a question, but in her heart Mary knew she was right.

"Probably," Samuel said, helping her down the slippery road.

They could barely see in front of them, but they knew the road well. When they arrived at the outskirts of the village, they could see the white, ghostly forms of others standing in the road ahead.

Kaboom, kaboom. The sound was like a heavy whisper.

"Is that you?" It was Mr. Evans who asked.

"Yes, Mr. Evans, with my brother."

"I'm afraid, I am, that all is lost." Mr. Evans looked toward the King's Highway as if he expected someone or something to walk out of the snow.

"Why dost thou say that?" Samuel asked.

"Samuel, you saw the army when they marched out of Princeton and crossed that bridge. They crossed the river to flee into Pennsylvania. Now that fool general has tried something risky. It can only fail." Mr. Evans turned his gaze down to the ground. "There's a garrison of Hessians in Trenton." Mr. Evans turned toward his house. He then spoke without looking back at them. "Come inside when you get too cold. Mrs. Evans will have hot coffee."

"Thanks to thee, Mr. Evans," Mary said. She watched him as he turned into a white shadow and then disappeared into the snow.

"They're silent."

Mary listened hard. All was still. Nothing came from it except the muffled voices from the villagers out listening and wondering. Minutes passed. Then one by one, head down, slowly the villagers retreated into their homes.

Mary longed for home. She nudged Samuel from his stance. Like the others in the village, they made their way home with a feeling that the Revolution had died on that morning.

For the rest of the day, Samuel was restless. With every sound heard coming from the road, he jumped up to peer out the window. Mrs. Stumpf, who was winding thread around a bobbin, would stop each time Samuel went to the window. Mary, sitting by the fire, pretended to read a book on farming. Like her mother, Samuel's bobbing up and down to the window distracted her. Mr. Stumpf sat with Paul in the kitchen writing out his plans for the crops come the spring. A horse's hooves were heard, clopping down the road. Samuel popped up again, following the rider from the front room window to the front kitchen window.

"Come," Paul said to Samuel. "We'll go out to the forge."

"And do what?" Samuel asked.

"The plow needs repairing."

Samuel hesitated. Paul took hold of Samuel's arm. "Come! Now before thou makest all insane with thy constant ups and downs."

"Go," Mr. Stumpf said.

The boys left the house. Mary joined her father at the table.

"Dad, this book has many ideas about the growing of fruit."

"Yes?"

The sound of a horse galloping toward the house interrupted Mary. Mr. Stumpf turned toward the sound. It slowed down to a trot, and then stopped. Human footsteps came to the front door, followed by a loud knock. Mr.

Stumpf jumped up to answer it, Mary close behind him. On the other side of the door a man stood. He was covered in a coat with his scarf over half his face and his hat pulled down nearly over his eyes. His horse stood in the yard.

"Good afternoon, sir. Are you Mister Stumpf?" the man said, pulling his scarf away. Mary could see he had not shaved for days.

"I am."

"My horse has thrown a shoe, and I am in a great deal of haste," the man continued.

"Art thou a messenger?" Mr. Stumpf said as he eyed the packet slung across the man's shoulder.

"I am."

Mr. Stumpf now reached for his coat and hat. "From the South?" he continued as he put on that coat.

"Yes sir, from Trenton I come."

"Oh sir, please tell us what has happened?" Mary rushed in.

"Why, young miss, Trenton is ours."

"Ours, whose?"

"General Washington led the troops there early this morning. Crossed the Delaware he did, and we have taken the town back. The Hessians are no more. Captured, nine hundred of 'em and taken to Pennsylvania."

Mary's jaw opened wide as she gasped. "I thank thee, sir," she said once she could remember to speak.

The man showed his smile and the twinkle of victory in his eye. "'Tis a grand day, lass, a grand day."

Nine

Victory

In the village of Stony Brook, Mr. Evans laughed aloud at nothing at all as he prepared his shop for customers. His son whistled as he swept the floor. Mr. Evans took time to dance a little gigue to the tune. Mary walked into the shop at this moment, astonished to see the usually restrained Mr. Evans executing a series of dance steps across the floor. Seeing her, Mr. Evans turned red with embarrassment. He quickly returned to his customary place behind the counter.

"It's a grand day, is it not, Mr. Evans?" Mary said.

"It is indeed." Mr. Evans peered closely at Mary. "It is indeed."

Mary smiled broadly at Mr. Evans. He gently nodded in response.

"What was that tune Edward whistled?"

"Edward?" Mr. Evans said to his son.

"Don't know, Mary. I heard it played at the Olden's Sunday last."

"He has a good ear for music," Mr. Evans said. "He can remember anything he hears."

"Wilt thou teach it to me?" Mary asked Edward.

"I will," Edward said as he began the tune again. Mary listened intensely, nodding her head to the rhythm of the song.

From the living quarter entryway came Suzanna. She had no smile nor did she dance, not even a little.

"Good morning," Suzanna said with a slight frown on her face. She spoke to no one in particular.

Edward briefly looked to his sister, and then increased his volume, sweeping closer to Suzanna. Mr. Evans waited, his hands now folded on the counter. Mary scrutinized Mr. Evan's face. He showed no emotion. Edward, however, teased Suzanna.

"Stop it!" Suzanna called out to Edward. "Your little dance means nothing to me."

"Edward," Mr. Evans commanded.

Edward stopped his whistling and his dance. He walked around to Mary, leaning over toward her ear as he did.

"She doesn't like it that we won," Edward whispered. Mary nodded. Edward picked up his dustbin to sweep up the trash into it.

"The thread?" Suzanna said looking directly at Mary.

"I have it," Mary said, bringing out several spools from the cloth bag she carried. Mary placed them, one at a time, on the counter, smiling at Mr. Evans, then at Edward, and finally, at Suzanna when the last spool came out of her bag. "Mother finished winding them last night." Mary turned back to Mr. Evans. "We were quite happy."

"Yes, we are, Mary, we all are. Such a sweet victory! Makes one wonder what the British think of us now." Mr. Evans stood up straight. "I admit I am a proud man on this day."

"I am as well," Edward said, taking the spools of thread to place them on the shelves.

"Not there," Suzanna said to Edward. "These are special ordered, for Mrs. Parker's dressmaker."

"Mrs. Parker? Bah!" Edward said.

"Are they promised?" Mr. Evans asked.

"Well, two of them," Suzanna said as she took two down from the shelf. "Mrs. Smyth will be in later this morning."

No sooner had the words come out of her mouth than Mary saw the Parker carriage pull up to the shop. They watched as the driver jumped down to open the carriage door for the robust Mrs. Smyth, Mrs. Parker's dressmaker. Suzanna rushed to the door to open it for her.

"Mrs. Parker would speak to you," Mrs. Smyth said to Suzanna as she crossed to the counter. Suzanna smiled as she left the shop. Mrs. Smyth gave a nod to Mr. Evans. "I'll take all that you have of the linen thread," she said.

"All? You are a prosperous tailor, Mrs. Smyth."

"The Parkers will entertain General Cornwallis and the others."

"Will they now?"

"Yes. They expect them within two days' time."

"As soon as that?" Mr. Evans frowned as he tallied up the prices for the spools.

"I am told General Cornwallis has orders to crush this rebellion once and for all. That General Howe was not happy with this turn of affairs." Mrs. Smyth read over the bill Mr. Evans handed her.

"There will be more fighting here?" Mary asked.

"Most likely." Mrs. Smyth smiled briefly at Mary, then turned her attention to the bill. "What of that linen cloth-have you any more?"

"Not in the shop. This is Mary Stumpf, the daughter of the woman responsible for that fine linen," Mr. Evans said, motioning toward Mary. "Have you linen for us, Mary?"

Mary wanted to lie, to say there was nothing for Mrs. Parker, for all she could remember was how Mr. Parker had treated her and Samuel. Instead, she said, "Some."

"How many yards would that some be?" Mrs. Smyth asked.

"Perhaps five."

"I'll take it. The carriage can take you home. Oh, of course, Mr. Evans, I will pay the shop price to you."

"I must ask my mother first, Mrs. Smyth. I may not promise anything."

"Then Suzanna will have to bring it round." Mrs. Smyth laid coins on the counter. She nodded her head to Mr. Evans. "Long live the king," she said before departing.

"Here, Mary, take your money," Mr. Evans said, handing the coins over to Mary. "I'll send Suzanna home with you." Mary nodded her head.

Suzanna had a smile on her face when she returned to the shop. "I've been invited to tea this afternoon, at the Parkers."

"First you'll go home with Mary to fetch some linen." Mr. Evans explained to her. Suzanna lost her smile for a time, but it returned broader than before.

Outside, Mary motioned to the still smiling girl to take the passenger seat in the cart. For a few moments, they held their peace as the horse trotted along the road. It was Suzanna who broke the silence.

"You are a Patriot."

"Why sayest thou that?"

"The way you smile, with Father." Suzanna smirked. "You are happy today, but in a few days' time…"

"Yes, I know. The Regulars will increase in numbers when Cornwallis arrives."

Suzanna pulled her cloak close to her body. "By the thousands."

"And this makes thee glad?"

"It does."

"Why then thy concern for Jimmy?"

"Jimmy?" Suzanna's face turned serious. She leaned forward, resting her head in her hands. "Jimmy is the most beautiful of all young men."

"This is thy regard for him?"

"Is it not for you?" She turned to see Mary looking at her. "Well?"

Mary said nothing. "Well?" Suzanna repeated.

"I'll not lie. Here is the fact. We wrote letters. But he has not written since November, and I am worried. Dost thou know anything about what might have happened to him?"

Suzanna looked straight ahead and fell silent. Mary looked to the girl, wondering why she did not answer. It came to her that Suzanna's silence admitted that Jimmy had not written to her: that her previous actions and questions had been nothing more than an attempt to know the relationship between Mary and Jimmy. As for anything there might have been between Jimmy and Suzanna, Mary concluded that Jimmy had kept his relationship with Suzanna limited. Suzanna pretended to more.

"Thou hast nothing to say?" Mary asked.

"Shall I find out?"

"How?"

"I have ways."

Mary turned suspicious. "Thou art loyal to the king, yes Suzanna?"

"I can be."

"*Can be?*"

"Oh Mary, I find all this bothersome. Tiresome. My father and Edward are all agog over this little victory. Mrs. Parker assures me this silly war will soon be over. In my mind, I know one side or the other shall win. Which side? I care not as long as my friendship with the Parkers is not harmed."

"Thou hast no loyalty?"

"None."

The cart pulled into the yard. Mary hopped out, going to the horse's head to hold him still. She watched Suzanna as she daintily stepped down. Mrs. Stumpf opened the door. Suzanna entered the house, leaving Mary to wait for her. Paul came out from the smithy.

"Dost thou need help with the cart or horse?" he asked Mary.

"No. But wait. Wilt thou drive Suzanna back?"

"I take it things are not happy between the two of you? No answer is needed." Paul grinned as he took the reins from Mary. "I'll drive her."

Mary sighed. "She seems without feeling or...."

"No explanation needed from thee to me, Mary. Go inside and fetch Dad's dinner. He will eat in the smithy today."

Mary kissed her elder brother on the cheek before returning to the house.

That night, as Mary lay in her bed, she took out the three letters Jimmy had written her. By the light of her one candle, she read each one. She sighed deeply as she folded and returned them to their place in the drawer. She snuggled down deep under her covers. How was Jimmy? Where was he? If he could, he would write, she told herself. The next thought she hated, because if he couldn't write he was someplace bad. Mary guessed that place to be New York. In what place in that distant city she dared not think about for she had heard too much about the prison ships anchored in the Hudson River. Without heat, these were awful places to keep prisoners. Mary stopped her thinking because those thoughts frightened her. She turned to face the windows. She wished the war were over, that no more soldiers would come to Stony Brook, or Trenton or Princeton. She prayed silently that this General Cornwallis would change his mind and leave the people alone.

Ten

Visitors

"They're here." Samuel took off his hat, and tossed it onto the hook by the kitchen door.

"Who?" Mary asked.

"The British, more Hessians, and…"

"Well?"

"Washington is back in Trenton."

"Better there than here."

A horse's hooves galloped by the house. Samuel ran to the front room, Mary following. By the time they peered out the window, the horse and rider were well down the road.

"Who was that?" Mary asked.

"I don't know. He wore no uniform."

"A spy!" Mary said it with glee.

"Mary? Samuel?" Mrs. Stumpf stood on the final stair that led to the front room. "Stay away from that window." She crossed to the kitchen door. "Mary, I see thou hast not packed the basket yet."

Mary moved quickly to the kitchen. She turned her attention to the basket that sat on the worktable. From the hutch she took down the items that had been prepared for their visit to their uncle's home in Maidenhead.

"Samuel, is thy brother to do all the packing of the wagon?" Mrs. Stumpf asked.

Samuel joined Paul at the wagon. This New Year's morning was cold, so they packed the wagon with jugs of hot water and blankets to keep them from freezing on the seven-mile journey. Mary brought out the basket she had filled with foodstuffs for the journey, breads, dried fruits and chunks of ham. The sound of more horses came from the north, this time two riders dressed in overcoats with scarves covering their faces. The riders urged their horses into a gallop.

"I should not think everyone goes to make merry today," Samuel said, his eyes following the horses as they ran round the bend in the road.

"I should think messengers don't make merry today," Paul said.

"Americans or British?" asked Mary.

"Could be either, though perhaps Americans bringing messages to Washington." Paul tied down the baskets so that they wouldn't bounce or move once they were on the road. "Samuel was in Princeton earlier. What did'st thou see?"

"How is that known to thee?" Samuel asked.

"Mr. Clarke stopped by to return the bridle thou lent him at sunup. Thou wast nowhere to be found, so I guessed thou wast in Princeton. Betwixt Mary," Paul looked toward Mary, "and thee, curiosity knows no bounds." Paul pulled the rope tight. "We are ready."

"Dost thou say we are gossips?" Samuel asked.

Paul scoffed. Mary put on her best innocent look. The siblings were then joined by their parents.

On their way to Maidenhead, several more riders passed them by. One wore the uniform of a British courier.

"Perhaps we should turn back?" Mrs. Stumpf suggested.

"No. We'll go as planned," Mr. Stumpf said.

Once they had arrived at their uncle's farm, the Stumpfs no longer paid attention to the activities on the road. The feasting commenced. All afternoon there was gaiety in the chatter. Mary's favorite cousin, Lazarus, showed her his many drawings of his family's farm, with several sketches of the calf, the chickens pecking, and his sister milking. Lazarus then drew Mary as she cut the cake she had baked into several pieces to pass around. When the sun dipped into the west, Mr. Stumpf announced that it was time for his family to return home before darkness. Paul and Samuel packed the wagon.

"Please, Father," Lazarus said to his parents, "may Mary stay the night?"

"Ask thine uncle."

Mary was given permission to stay. Along with her cousins, her uncle, and her aunt, she waved goodbye to her parents and brothers.

The next morning, Lazarus and Mary mounted horses to take a ride to visit their various friends in the area. They took to the King's Highway, stopping off here and there until nearly dinnertime. They pushed farther south to dine with another uncle. On their way there, they passed Americans digging up the roadway and setting up guns.

"What are you doing here?" Lazarus asked of the soldiers.

"Well, young man, in a few hours, thousands of British and Hessian soldiers will march down that road on their way to Trenton."

"Then 'tis true," Mary said. "Just as my brother said it would be."

"Yes, young miss."

"What will you do, fire on them?" Lazarus asked.

"Yes, we will."

"But if there are thousands of them…" Lazarus's voice trailed off as he looked over the soldiers preparing for battle. There were many of them, but not thousands.

"Never you mind that," the soldier said. "Best you two get back to your home. It won't be safe for you here."

"We're on our way to that farm yonder," Lazarus said as he pointed with his chin to his uncle's farmhouse in the distance.

"Then get yourself there, and stay there." The soldier stopped digging to look sternly up at the two cousins.

The excitement of the moment rushed through Mary's veins. She felt both curious and frightened. She turned her horse toward her uncle's farmhouse, but Lazarus didn't follow. The sight of the soldiers working captured him. Mary turned back, leaned over, and took hold of Lazarus's reins.

"We can see the soldiers from Uncle's house," Mary whispered to Lazarus.

"Yes, that's true."

They urged their horses into a canter so that they could arrive quickly. Their Uncle Henry, a thin man of middling height, ran out of the house to greet them.

"Hurry, the both of ye, for the British will be here soon. Those soldiers will fire upon them, and violence of this nature knows no boundaries. No boundaries!" He said it as he quickly shoved Mary and Lazarus inside the house.

"Can't we watch from here?" Mary asked.

"Watch? Men shooting at one another with stray bullets coming our way?" Their uncle now led them to the back of the house, where the kitchen was located. "You stay inside."

"Into the cellar," their Aunt Dorothea commanded. "There is safety there."

Aunt Dorothea was a small, yet robust woman of thirty. She was the mother of five children, one an infant not yet six months old. Nothing got past Dorothea. Nothing. She was to be obeyed, and so Mary and Lazarus made their way down to the cellar. There they found their cousins seated at the kitchen table, which had been set up there, complete with food, drink, and chairs to sit on. Aunt Dorothea soon followed with a stack of blankets, one for everyone present. Mary welcomed its warmth, for the cellar was cold.

"When dost thou think it will begin?" asked the eldest cousin, Joshua, who was just eight years of age.

"I don't know," said Lazarus. "We shall have to wait and see."

They didn't have long to wait. After twenty minutes, the first shot rang out. The baby, startled, burst into tears. Mary's mouth fell open. It was one thing to see men preparing for a battle and quite another to hear it. She didn't know what to expect, or if they would be safe. This would not be like the soldier who had died in the brook. Many soldiers could die, including the recently spoken to Americans.

More shots rang out. The baby started to scream, and Aunt Dorothea picked her up to sooth her. It helped somewhat, but the cellar was becoming a noisy place. Without excusing herself, Mary jumped up from the table, grabbed her chair, and dragged it to the high, narrow windows that were at ground level on the outside of the house. There she placed her chair, so that by standing on it, so she could peek out.

"Get down from there!" Uncle Henry commanded.

"Soon," she said, blatantly disobeying. Mary's curiosity took control of her very being. She could not stand down from that window any more than she could stop the action outside. She watched in fascination as the British soldiers arrived near the dug in Americans. From their earthworks, the Americans fired en masse on the approaching British. Mary's jaw fell open as she watched the men struck by bullets fall.

Uncle Henry, whose attention was taken by his younger children, all who seemed to be crying or shaking or both, left Mary to watch out the window. It was real, this skirmish. Not a story read from a book, or reported by an old soldier. From her viewing post she saw men wounded, perhaps killed. Fortunately, she was too far away to know one way or the other. Soldiers stopped to pick up many of their fallen comrades. They helped the wounded to safety. She turned her eyes to see that the Americans were so well protected they did not have the casualties the British had.

This held for only a short time. As more, and still more, British soldiers arrived on the scene, the Americans had to pull back. Using the shrubs, trees, and a bend in the road for cover, they fired on the British, then pulled back to hide on either side of the road. Mary watched in awe as one American soldier fired from the side of a tree right near the house. As soon as he fired his gun, he stepped around to the back of the tree to reload his weapon and then fire again. Mary turned her attention back to the British line. They were stopped. They dared not move forward. That is when Uncle Henry grabbed her from behind.

"Didst thou not hear me, Mary?" he said, pulling her from her perch.

"But I would watch!" she cried out.

Henry swung Mary around to carry her and the chair back to the table. Mary saw the look of horror on Dorothea's face as her aunt studied her attitude of offending disobedience. Mary's defiance plus a desire to watch the dreadful horrified them.

On Mary's part, it was more than a fascination for the act of war that kept her pinned to the window. Men fighting for *something*, for an idea, reminded her of what Jimmy had said to her as he left to join the Continental Army. This act of fighting, for this idea of America, displayed itself out there on the King's Highway. Right here, near her uncle's farm, was the sort of men who fought for that belief. They risked their lives for it. Some would die. This train of thought pulled Mary's attention back to the window.

Outside, the gunfire grew ever more intense. Henry closed his eyes. Mary knew he prayed, for his lips moved. It was to no avail because the firing increased.

"They're very close," he said, opening his eyes.

His listening proved acute, for soon they heard footsteps run across the yard. Human legs soon came into sight. Horses galloped by. More shots fired. Broad, loud snaps repeating, one on top of the other.

A man's voice boomed out in German, "*Schmutzige, faule Rebellen!*"

Dorothea understood the German language. She turned white. Her breathing quickened, the color returned to her face as she grew angry. She muttered under her breath, "How dare you call them rotten rebels!" Dorothea stood up, and handed the baby to her husband. "*Sie schmutziger Hesse, gehen Sie zu Ihrem Land zurück!*" she shouted as she ran to the window.

"Dorothea!" Henry cried out to his wife. "Sit down!"

Instead of following her husband's command, Dorothea turned abruptly around, glared at him, and then just as abruptly marched across the cellar to the rear door that led out to the yard. Henry stood, holding up the crying infant.

"*Sie setzen sich,*" Dorothea said forcefully as she threw open the door.

Mary's jaw dropped nearly to the ground. Without a thought, Dorothea now ran out into the yard. Mary hesitated only for a moment before she followed her aunt.

Henry screeched behind her, "Dorothea!" All the children screamed, the baby at the top of her lungs. Not to be left out, Lazarus soon joined Mary and Dorothea.

84

In the yard and beyond were soldiers firing, the Americans well hidden and moving southwest, and the Hessians taking cover, firing, and then moving ahead only to be stopped by the Americans returning their fire.

"Aunt Dorothea!" Lazarus shouted out as a Hessian officer on a horse galloped their way.

Dorothea stopped in the middle of the yard, and held up her fist at the Hessian officer who reined in his horse. She took another step toward the officer.

"Lady!" he said without much of an accent. "Go back!"

"*Ich? Das ist meine Farm. Sie gehen zurück. Gehen Sie!*"

The Hessian officer looked astounded by the woman standing firm. Somewhere an old memory must have reminded himself of his own mother scolding him, for he backed his horse away. Dorothea, in her determination, kept coming at him. Three other Hessians now joined him. The officer said something to them, but the words were lost, drowned out by the loudness of the fight around them.

Mary took the moment to run to Dorothea. She placed her arm around her aunt's waist. The officer now confronted with two women, one quite young, turned back to say something to his men. Mary thought he looked perplexed. He turned back to the stone-faced Dorothea.

"Lady, I am a soldier. No war on women and children. You understand? *Sie verstehen?*"

Mary, listening to a voice inside her, decided it would be best to intervene.

"Come, Aunt," Mary said, using her arm to direct her aunt back to the house. Dorothea was reluctant at first. She hadn't finished staring angrily at the officer.

Mary could see from the officer's expression that he was grateful for Mary's intervention. He saluted Dorothea with a grand sweep of his hat. He then gave Mary a nod before he rode off with the others. With Lazarus's help, they directed Dorothea back to the cellar door. When the three of them reached the bottom of the steps, Henry burst into tears in gratitude that none were killed. He felt Dorothea's and then Mary's arms. He checked Lazarus's head. Finding everyone whole, he motioned to the three to return to their seats. He had taken out a bottle of Madeira wine. He now poured the wine, giving even Mary and Lazarus a glass of the fine drink.

By the time they had finished the wine, the sounds of the skirmishes grew distant. Mary stared straight ahead, the wine calming her. It was a day she would never forget for it had been exciting, upsetting and revealing to her. Upstairs, the clock chimed two. In two hours, it would be dark. Mary was alarmed. She needed to think about leaving, as her parents expected her home by sundown. Mary leaned over to say this to Lazarus as a gun fired close by. A thud followed. They all turned their attention to the cellar window in time to see the body of the German officer flip over and nearly crash into the glass.

Everyone gasped. In moments, as they watched in horror, life left his face.

Eleven

Escape

"Go into the kitchen. All of you," Henry said. "Mary and Lazarus, I will saddle your horses. When I call you, come outside."

"Yes Uncle," Mary and Lazarus said in unison.

Led by their aunt, Mary followed her cousins up the cellar stairs. Henry stood motionless, watching them, until they had disappeared into the kitchen. Mary, who slowly closed the door to the cellar, saw her uncle leave by the door they had used to confront the Hessians.

Dorothea stoked the fire. In the distance, cannon fired. Dorothea shook her head, but said nothing.

"It's begun," Lazarus whispered to Mary. "The battle in Trenton."

Mary nodded her head.

"Sit," Dorothea said to all the cousins.

Dorothea's children obeyed her. Mary did not feel like sitting down, so she stood by the back window. She watched as Henry dragged the body of the Hessian officer away from the house, toward the front drive. He then disappeared from her view.

"At least the baby sleeps," Dorothea said. "Children, you must be hungry. Martha, take out some bread." Martha rapidly obeyed her mother.

Dorothea gave the baby to Mary. "I'll prepare for thee bread with butter and jam for thy ride home, Mary."

"I thank thee, Aunt."

"I am sorry for my actions and beg thy forgiveness, Mary."

"'There is no need, Aunt."

The cannon fire was now incessant. Dorothea glanced out the door, looking south toward Trenton. "Another battle. God help them."

"Sounds like Trenton," Joshua said.

"So many have left Trenton to stay with relatives elsewhere. I pray they have homes to return to." Dorothea turned to cutting bread and spreading butter and jam across the slices. "Today was close enough. No more, please Lord, no more." Dorothea wrapped the slices in pieces of linen. This she handed to Mary. "Be careful, be very, very careful. Both of you."

"Yes, Aunt. We promise," Mary said.

Henry returned to the house. "Mary, Lazarus, come with me."

Outside, the saddled horses waited for Mary and Lazarus by the barn. They mounted their steeds, and pointed them toward the road.

"Stay away from the soldiers," Henry told them. "The road is very muddy, nearly impassable. Keep to the side. It's firmer there."

Mary and Lazarus nodded.

"Now go. I would go with you, but I cannot leave my family."

"We understand, Uncle," Lazarus said. "We will do as you say." He turned his horse east toward the King's Highway. Mary followed.

When they reached the end of the drive, they saw the dead Hessian lying by the side of the road, his horse tied to the fence nearby. His eyes had been shut, and his hands were crossed across his chest. Blood still slowly flowed out of the side of his chest. Mary quickly looked away from the officer. She had never experienced death like this, where someone she had faced was killed violently and now lay dead, laid out without the benefit of a shroud or a pine box to hold his lifeless body.

Lazarus stopped his horse to look the Hessian officer over.

"Why dost thou stop?" Mary asked.

"I wish I could draw him."

"Why?"

"Father says death is a part of life, and there is nothing of life I wouldn't draw, Mary. Nothing."

"Then I am glad we must hurry." Mary urged her horse forward as she turned north on the highway. As per her uncle's instructions, she moved the beast to the side where the mud was not as deep or gummy as that in the middle of the road. Ahead, Mary could see British soldiers picking up the wounded or the dead along the highway. "Come, Lazarus, here are soldiers. Let's be gone."

"Yes, yes." Lazarus followed Mary up the road. The debris left behind by the conflict now took up his interest. Spent balls were everywhere. Pieces of bloodied clothing, belts, a horseshoe, and wood pieces from a broken wagon wheel were scattered here and there. Lazarus reached down to his saddlebag to take out the sketchbook he carried with him, but quickly changed his mind. The soldiers were coming closer.

"Should we speak to them?" Lazarus asked.

"No. Only if spoken to."

In a few moments more, they were within earshot of the soldiers' conversation.

"Come on, lads, hurry it up or it will be dark before we get to the battle," one of the soldiers in charge said.

"Sounds like they're in the thick of it," another replied.

"Here!" The British Regular looked straight at Mary and Lazarus. "Where do you two think you're going?"

"Home." Lazarus said without stopping.

"Better be quick about it. We don't know what lurks about."

"Yes sir. We'll be quick." Lazarus urged his horse into a trot, and Mary did the same.

After they had gone some way in silence, Lazarus said, "I don't think they meant us any harm."

"Thou art young yet. Too young to be a soldier. If thou wast Jimmy…"

"Jimmy? Samuel's friend?"

"Yes, Samuel's friend."

"Even Samuel riding with us might not be a good idea."

Mary hadn't thought of that. Odd, she thought, that she should have to think of protecting her brothers. She remembered how her mother had protected them, all of her family, from the prying British officer who wanted to know if they had seen anyone by the brook near their house.

"Samuel never speaks of Jimmy. At least not to me," Lazarus said.

"No?"

"Not since he joined the army."

"I've had three letters from him. Nothing more."

"He writes to you?" Lazarus said it with some excitement.

"When he can."

"What does he say?"

"What we know. New York fell to the British. Perhaps now Trenton will as well."

Lazarus turned his head back toward the south. "Who knows?"

Mary shrugged her shoulders. The air was growing chilly. She pulled her cloak up around her. It would be a cold night. She kicked her horse's side, and he broke into a canter. It wasn't long before they turned the final bend in the road and found themselves back at Lazarus's family's farm. There they found Mr. Stumpf mounted on a horse, preparing to ride south in search of his daughter and nephew. Mary was relieved and happy to see her father. Mr. Stumpf smiled broadly.

"We feared the worst!" Lazarus's father said, running out to the road. "Look, thy father is here to take thee home, Mary."

Mary leaned across her horse to hug her father, who held her tightly in his embrace.

"Art thou well, Mary?" Mr. Stumpf asked.

"I am." She leaned back to face him. "I have seen much today that I shall never forget." She wanted to cry.

She stopped herself. Instead, she returned her father's smile.

"Come then, let's go home. Thy mother is beside herself with worry."

Before he turned his horse to ride north, Mr. Stumpf stopped to listen to the sounds of battle coming from the distance.

"They fight late in Trenton," Lazarus said.

"So they do," Mr. Stumpf said, "Good evening," he said, urging his horse eastward, toward Stony Brook.

Father and daughter rode away as the sun was nearing the horizon, and they had seven miles to ride before they could be home. Before long, they broke into a gentle canter, which brought them home just as the sun slipped away. With the sun gone, the air turned frigid.

"Mary! Mary!" Her mother ran out of the house to throw her arms around her as she dismounted.

"Mother! I am so happy to be home!"

No matter how grand the adventure, Mary now felt that home was the best place to be. At supper, the family gathered in the kitchen, around the table, with only the light of the fireplace reflecting on their faces. They sat, held their moment of silence, and when finished, all seemed to speak at once as they dipped bread into a hot soup to fill their bellies with the nourishing bounty of the Jerseys.

"Didst thou see Lord Cornwallis, Mary?" Samuel asked.

"No, I didn't."

"They were having a difficult time of it; the roads were muddy," Samuel continued with a smile on his face. "All those well supplied soldiers of His Majesty's forces brought to their knees by the weather."

"We heard firing along the highway," Paul said. "Where wast thou?"

"At Uncle Henry's."

Mary then related some of her story to her family, but left out the part where Aunt Dorothea confronted the Hessian and how, later, that Hessian died.

Mrs. Stumpf grew pale as Mary spoke. "Thou wast in danger! Thy life could have been taken!" she blurted out and then broke into tears.

"Perhaps we best tell these tales some other time." Mr. Stumpf looked from face to face to see if all had heard him. "The armies fight it out in Trenton, Miriam. Pray they stay there."

After supper, Mary went out to the barn to take slop to the pigs and to see the cows and chickens. In spite of the frigid chill, she decided to walk through her orchard. She ran her hands along the bark, going from tree to tree, traveling up one side and then another. How she loved this place. How she loved their farm. She paused to take in a deep breath. The air was fresh and crisp. She turned to face south. She could hear nothing coming from Trenton. The soldiers, she guessed, had bedded down for the night. It had been a long day for them. It had been a long day for her as well.

Mary sat on the fence. She looked up at the stars that shone brilliantly on that moonless night. Like sparkling jewels on a wealthy lady, the stars dazzled her. At that moment, Mary felt, for the first time in her life, her uniqueness, her separateness. She turned to look at the house. The lights coming from the other windows meant her family sat in the front room. She wanted to join them, but stopped herself.

Something about this day, about this night, was teaching her. What, she could not put her finger on. Right now, it was nothing more than a feeling she had. She returned to looking at the sky. It was vast. It was limitless. The stars winked at her in a sly way that told her they knew the answer to her question.

"Do ye know, little stars, what it is I feel?" Mary said. "But why not say, why not tell me?" The stars were silent.

Mary looked back at the house. Inside its walls, she belonged to something that was greater than her. She jumped off the fence for she felt compelled to return to its warmth. She no longer wanted to be alone with her thoughts, which seemed to match the vastness of the sky. The cold and the adventuresome day had taken its toll as well.

In the kitchen, Mary filled the bed warmer with red coals from the fireplace. She crossed to the steps, and from the bottom step said, "Good night," to her family gathered around the fire.

"Good night," they said.

Upstairs, Mary passed the bed warmer several times over the linens. When her sheets were warm, she drew up the feather comforter to seal in the heat. Quickly, she undressed and snuggled under the covers. It was warm, and cozy, Mary was warm and cozy. Her eyelids grew heavy.

The last thing she remembered was saying good night to a radiant star that seemingly winked at her.

Miles away from where Mary slept safely in her bed, American soldiers in Trenton did not take to their beds. As fatigued as they were from fortifying their position on Mill Hill all morning, as tired as they were from fighting off wave upon wave of British and Hessian soldiers who had attempted to cross over the Assunpink Bridge and take the American position on Mill Hill, the American army's work was not finished. Darkness did not bring a halt to anything.

General Cornwallis's army could sleep while Mary slept. General Washington's army did not. Their general planned something extraordinary. As Mary turned in her warm bed, American soldiers added wood to the huge bonfires that burned all along the Assunpink gorge. The American soldiers greased the wheels of their wagons and wrapped their horses' hooves with rags. While Mary slipped into a deep sleep, the Continental Army slipped away from the British and Hessians.

Twelve

Battle

Mary dreamed.

In her dream, hundreds of soldiers were everywhere. In the fields, on the roads, in boats floating down a river, men dressed in uniforms carried long guns or dragged cannon to fire on one another.

"Mary!" she thought she heard. She turned toward the sound. No one spoke. Even when the soldiers fired their weapons they had no sound to them.

"Mary!" It came again.

Again she turned. Again, silence.

It turned dark. Very dark. The soldiers were outlines in vivid colors against the blackness of the night sky. Whatever their movements were, they had no faces, only uniforms that floated down a river or marched in circles.

"Mary! Ma-ma-ry! Ma-ma-ry!"

Mary grew frightened. The quality of the dream was turning nightmarish.

"Ma-ma-ry-ry! Ma-ma-ry-ry! Ma-ma-ry-ry!" The voice was rhythmic in its repetition. The sound then changed, but not its rhythm.

Ta-ta-ta-tah. Ta-ta-ta-tah. Ta-ta-ta-tah. She did not recognize the drumbeat.

The soldiers melted into the darkness. Then, from the corner of the canvas of the dream, a small light grew visible. It grew larger, larger, until she could see the form of a drummer boy beating his drum. The boy wore a black hat, and underneath that hat, he had long blond hair tied back with a black ribbon. She could not see his face because he looked down to his drum. Only the top of his hat and his formless chin were visible to her.

She tried to call out to the drummer. She formed the word, but there was no sound. She tried again. Slowly, she pushed her tongue to her palette to form a "j", but she could not speak. Frustrated as she was, Mary would try again. "Ji-mm-y," she formed in her mouth.

She heard nothing. Her frustration grew as she attempted to call out several times. Something, it seemed, held her down. There was a weight in her throat, on her arms, in her feet. She struggled. The more she struggled, the more she became bogged down. Still she would not give up.

"Jim-my!" No sound.

"J-i-mm-y!" No sound. With a Herculean effort, she forced her lips to move. Now she focused all of her energy into her mouth.

"Ji...ji...JIMMY!"

No sooner had she said it than the sound of her voice came back to her. Stillness followed as the drummer lifted his face. It was not Jimmy at all, but the Hessian officer, his dead eyes staring at her.

Mary gasped as she woke. She sat up in her bed. She was cold. In the pitch darkness of the room, she felt for her comforter. It was not on her bed. She reached down to feel for it on the floor. Finding it she dragged it back up to the bed to cover her body. She shivered for several moments before she felt herself turning warm.

"Dear God, dear God, what does this dream mean?" she whispered.

The clock in the front room struck 1 am. Mary turned toward her windows. A new set of stars stood at attention against the black sky. Perhaps, she thought, she should have told her parents about the dead Hessian. That, she argued with herself, would only have upset them more than they had been. She turned away from the windows. The stars provoked too much thought.

On the dark wall ahead of her, she tried to form an image of Jimmy's face against it. All she saw was his golden hair, shimmering in the darkness.

"Jimmy," she whispered. "Where art thou?" She was desperate to recall his face, as she had left him all those months back, with him smiling down at her. She closed her eyes to remember. She could feel herself smiling, remembering their farewell. It was strange to her that after the fright of the dream, this past sorrowful moment of Jimmy's leaving should now seem so sweet.

Mary lay back down in the warmth of her bed. Her beating heart returned to its normal pace as her eyelids grew heavy. She sighed as the warmth pulled her along into slumber.

Miles away, General Washington rode his proud horse at the head of his men. He wished for a warm bed, but there would be none this night. Not for him nor any of the men who followed him as they marched to the next stop on this road of destiny. That destiny included not only this weary, determined army, but a girl who lay dreaming about an American soldier.

At 7 am, the rooster on the Stumpf farm crowed loudly. Mary's eyes popped open. Something or someone was outside. She listened for the rooster to crow again. Instead, she heard a muffled sound that was rhythmic. *Shwootshwootshwoot...* was followed by a *rooohrooooh...* interspersed within the *shwoots*.

Mary slowly raised her head. Men were marching outside her window! She bounded up and across to it. On the road below, hundreds of soldiers were passing by. She recognized them. They were Americans. They had cannons with wheels wrapped in rags. Horses' hooves were also wrapped in pieces of cloth. Among themselves, the men said nothing.

Without giving it a second thought, Mary grabbed her clothes, ran out of her room, down the stairs. She crossed to the kitchen, but then stopped. There in the front room was Samuel seated in front of the fire that roared.

"What took thee so long?"

Mary was astonished, but said nothing.

"Speechless? Good. Get thee into the kitchen where the fire waits for thee to dress."

Mary ran into the kitchen to see the fire blazing in there as well. Spread out on a bench in front of the fire was Mary's cloak. Mary smiled broadly. She jumped into her clothing as fast as she could.

"They've stopped," Samuel whispered loudly from the front window.

Mary threw on her warmed cloak. "Let's go."

"The question is where?"

"They will tell us."

"They will tell us to get back inside." Samuel smiled as he waved to a soldier who had seen him looking out the window. "Come. Out the back."

He turned away and headed through the kitchen. Mary followed. Stealthily, they went out to the barnyard where they could see the soldiers lined up on the road that curved round the back of their barn. Mary and Samuel entered the barn. Inside, they waited a moment before they crossed to the north side doors. They opened it in time to see the front line of soldiers moving off. Sitting atop his horse was General Washington.

"Why it's Washington," Samuel said.

"Yes."

"Something big is here, Mary."

"We should follow."

"We can go through the back woods."

Just then a second group of soldiers moved west.

"Wait. Where are they going?" asked Mary.

"I don't know. We can't follow both." Samuel mused for a moment. "I say we follow Washington."

"Agreed." Mary reached down to grab a bucket in one hand, and then reached up to take a scythe in the other. "Here, we'll pretend to do chores."

"A scythe in the middle of winter?"

Mary returned the scythe to its place. Instead, she picked up the second bucket.

"Thou must go first, as if to feed the pigs. When thou hast opportunity, disappear into the woods. I will then follow."

Samuel did as Mary said. Mary noticed a soldier following Samuel's movements with his eyes. She wondered what she should do, but then the soldier moved on ahead. He could no longer see Samuel. When Samuel walked into the woods, Mary waited a moment before coming out of the barn.

"Ye!" a voice from the soldiers called out.

Mary turned toward the voice to see an officer seated on a horse. He was well dressed with a youngish face.

"Yes?" Mary said

"Go back inside."

"I have to feed the pigs," Mary explained as she walked toward him.

"Nay, get ye back inside."

"General Mercer, sir," a soldier said as he ran up to the officer seated on the horse.

"Aye, what is it?"

Mary took the opportunity of this General Mercer's distraction to run off into the woods. She found Samuel kneeling behind a tree, watching the soldiers march off toward the Meeting House.

"They've reached the Meeting House." Samuel spoke in a whisper.

"How dost thou know that?" Mary too whispered.

"By the length of the line."

They both watched in silence as the line of soldiers proceeded northeast.

"Look!" Samuel said as he turned his face southwest. "There's the end. As soon as they disappear around the bend, we'll run across and cut through to the Meeting House."

Mary nodded in agreement. It took another five minutes for the last of the marching troops to reach the bend. In another five minutes, they were gone. Samuel walked to the edge of the road. He glanced up and then down. He could see no one left.

"Come on, Mary."

The two raced across the road, across the fields, and in minutes, found themselves by their Meeting House. The small stoned house was quiet and dark. Mary and Samuel stopped on its front porch.

"What dost thou think will happen?" Mary said.

"They are on their way to Nassau Hall. There are British soldiers there and the prisoners. Why, there must be guns and cannon and such... Yes, we can use those items."

Mary's eyes followed the distant line of Americans. Something bright then flashed into her eyes.

"What is that?"

"What?"

"Who are those soldiers?"

"Where?"

Mary pointed to the hill across the way. Hundreds of British soldiers were running down the hill.

"They're going toward William Clarke's farm!" Samuel shouted. "Come Mary, quick, let's go to Thomas' farm."

"We should return home!" Mary grabbed hold of Samuel's arm, pulling him back. "There's going to be a battle. Don't go. It's an awful thing to see men die!"

Samuel looked at her quizzically. "What dost thou mean, Mary? What hast thou seen?"

Mary kept her silence. She looked away from Samuel, for she did not want to feel compelled to tell him of the incident with the Hessian officer. Samuel crossed the road to the Meeting House. Mary remained where she was. It was then the first shots rang out. Samuel froze to the spot. He looked toward the sound. More shots rang out. Samuel turned to look back at Mary who pleaded with him with her eyes to not do what he was bound to do. Samuel stayed motionless for only a second. While Mary watched, he ran up the hill toward Thomas Clarke's farm. She soon followed.

When they found themselves in front of Thomas's big barn, they could see soldiers running here and there.

"It's a battle, Mary!"

"Samuel—" Mary meant to say more, meant to reach out to Samuel to pull him back toward the Meeting House, but found that she, too, was captivated. She stood in the road as if in a trance amidst the chaos of a battle just begun.

"Mary?"

"Samuel, this is madness." She said it without emotion. Out of the corner of her eye she saw Samuel approach the corner of the large barn. She knew what he would do. He would creep along its edge until he got to the back of the building. There he could see the fields, and there, Mary guessed, was where the fighting would take place.

The noise of the gunfire grew louder. Men were now yelling out to one another. Mary joined Samuel to creep along the edge of the barn. When they reached the end of the southern wall, the angle was wrong, and they could see only a few soldiers who seemed to be running from the field, not onto it.

"The carriage barn!" Samuel shouted out over the noise of the battle.

Mary had already turned back to retrace her steps out to the road. She then ran up the road and over to the corner of the smaller barn. She edged along its front, toward the house. She was so intent; she didn't notice anyone approach until she felt a strong hand grab hold of her arm.

"Where do you think you're going?" the stern male voice said.

Mary wheeled around to see a soldier wearing a green uniform looking her squarely in the eyes. His eyes were gray, fierce, and penetrating.

"To see...to see-"

"Captain!"

It was another male voice. Mary turned her face toward it. A young black man, also in a green uniform and tall enough to handle Samuel, was dragging her brother toward her.

"Captain, here's another one."

"You know him?" the captain asked Mary.

"My brother."

"Peter, let's put them in here," the captain said as he ushered Mary through the carriage barn door. Once inside, he sat Mary down on a stool. "Stay there. You, too," he said to Samuel. "Get down, both of you, and don't move from this corner."

The captain left the barn.

"You heard what Captain Shippin said," said the man named Peter. "It's dangerous, even in here. So just stay until we come after you. Promise."

"Yes sir," Mary said.

Samuel gave a sullen nod of the head. Peter left the barn. The gunfire grew ever more loud. Mary looked around the interior of the barn. Once her eyes had become accustomed to the darkness, she saw that there were two nervous horses and a wagon. Near the back doors, she noted a ladder that led to the loft. She elbowed Samuel and pointed. He saw it. It did not take him long to leave the place of safety for the ladder.

In moments, they were in the loft. At its western end was a door used for tossing hay and straw out to the ground below. It was closed. Around the door's edge, light was streaming in. Mary and Samuel stared at it with longing. On the other side lay a world unknown to them, enticing them to explore it.

For how long they stayed still in the center of that loft they would never be able to tell. Seconds or minutes, it seemed an eternity. Then, slowly, they crawled to the door. There they would do what they wanted to do. They opened the door.

Thirteen

A View of All Things

There, before them, in its awful splendor, was the great scene. Down the hill, spread out on Thomas Clarke's farm across to his brother William's orchard, were British soldiers. Hundreds of them, some on foot, some on horse, while others stood behind pieces of artillery they had hurriedly set up at the bottom of the hill.

From around Thomas's house, and across William's fields, the Americans gathered, running with all their might to form their own lines of battle facing the British. Their artillerymen formed a line of cannon just below Thomas's house, near the top of the hill. They worked speedily to set up their huge guns, load them, and return fire.

Mary wondered about the men who were below her. What sort of conviction allowed them to face their enemy at such close range? The idea, she mused again, the idea of America compelled these men to stand on this field of battle, to risk all for the sake of a nation that was only a dream. Was this, she asked in her heart, the way ideas, that seemed fanciful to some, became real for the person who conceived them? Did all ideas need such violence to bring them to fruition?

The scene before her worked its way deeply into her mind.

"Look there, to the right!" Samuel shouted.

More American soldiers ran across William Clarke's fields. Some seemed hesitant. Others were itching for a fight. Then, in a moment forever fixed in Mary's mind, General Washington dashed out onto the field. He stopped his horse so suddenly that it reared up.

Coming toward Washington were soldiers who tried to run off the fields. He stopped them and leaned down to speak to them.

"There are more of us than them! This day can be ours! Go back!" Washington said.

He turned his horse around and headed back toward the center of the fields. The men who had been running away followed him. In minutes, the soldiers of both sides lined up in a long arc that spread across from Thomas Clarke's house through William Clarke's fields.

Mary surveyed each side, and realized that Washington left himself in a precarious position.

"He could be shot," she shouted out to Samuel.

"He leads his troops, Mary. They were scared. He's not."

Each side then opened fire. *Kaboom!* went the cannons. The barn shook. Smoke from all the various guns fired at once rose up and clouded the view. More shots fired, and then more cannon spit their balls across the field.

Captain Shippin and Peter, among others dressed in the same green uniforms, kneeled down, prepared to fire. Across the field many yards away, the British commander rode down the line of his men, shouting out orders. They quickly shifted their lines, the front line kneeled down, ready to fire.

Washington commanded his men, riding his horse in and among them. The front line of the Americans now knelt. They, too, were prepared to fire their weapons.

"Why isn't the general more careful?" Mary cried out.

No sooner had she spoken than every soldier kneeling on the front lines, and every artillery man standing by his cannon, fired. The noise of it was deafening. Mary covered her ears but kept her eyes focused on the scene below.

Smoke filled the air as the thousands of guns fired, the front row of men reloading while the second row fired. This scene of human violence seemed to play out in a fog. The soldiers in William Clarke's field were lost in it.

"I can't see them! Are they still there? And where is he?"

"Who?"

"Washington!"

Samuel shook his head. It was impossible to see anything until the smoke should lift a bit. The soldiers below, however, reloaded and fired so quickly that the smoke of the gunpowder increased in this intense battle.

Mary turned her attention to the far fields. She strained to see what the soldiers did there. She leaned out, grabbing onto the hayloft door to steady her. Suddenly, the artillery fired with such fierceness that the barn shook to its foundation. The door moved out, pulling Mary's body with it. She screamed.

Samuel reacted swiftly. He took hold of Mary's cloak, keeping her from falling to the ground. Bracing himself against the doorframe with his feet, Samuel pulled Mary back into the loft.

"Stay inside!" Samuel roared.

He would not have to tell her a second time.

The smoke now drifted up to the barn's doorway. They waved it away, though that helped but little. The air was so still on that frosty morning that the smoke hugged it. Little by little, it dispersed as the soldiers shifted their lines. That's when Mary saw him, Washington, still sitting on top of his horse, in command of his men and of himself. Next to him was another man, also on horseback. It was the same black man that Mary had seen riding with Washington when they had crossed the Stony Brook at the bridge with the mill, and rode beside him when Washington led the men toward Princeton.

After minutes of repeated firings, a great shout went up from the Americans below. The British soldiers were moving back, retreating. The Americans put ever more pressure on them, moving in to win the battle.

"They're running!" shouted Samuel. "They're giving up!"

What had started as an orderly withdrawal soon turned into a rout. The British line broke, and off they went, off Thomas's fields to make a mad dash up the hill toward the King's Highway. Hundreds of Americans chased them. After a short pursuit of the enemy, Washington returned to organize his men again, this time to continue their march north and east.

"They'll go to Nassau Hall and release the prisoners." Samuel leaned back on his heels. "To think, Mary, that these men marched all night, did battle, and now will fight again, and then…"

"And then, what?"

"They will have to leave town."

"Because that general, Cornwallis, will have discovered they are no longer in Trenton." Mary kept her eyes wandering over the field below. "What of these wounded?"

"They will be cared for." Samuel said it while observing the after battle actions below him. He watched as an American officer spoke to four artillerymen who stood around a cannon. "Those men," Samuel pointed them out, "will go to the bridge."

"Why to the bridge?"

"Cornwallis will want to cross that bridge, Mary."

"I understand. Like yesterday, the Americans will hold the British soldiers back. But where will Washington lead his army?"

"I don't know."

They were silent, intent on the view before them. And then Samuel stood.

"This is a great victory for us, Mary. We have won," he said with a look of glee over his face. "First against the Hessians, and now against the British. I am hopeful, Mary. I am hopeful. Dost thou hear me?"

Mary stared at something out on the field. A silver epaulette caught in the morning's sun sparkled on the ground. Mary gasped when she realized what it was.

"I have to get down," she said.

"No. Wait for the captain."

"He's not coming." She pointed toward the body with the silver epaulette.

"That's a long way off, Mary. How can'st thou know who that is?"

"The silver. See?" Mary patted her shoulder.

Samuel studied the scene in the distance. After a moment he nodded, pushing himself up from the floor and away from the door.

"Let's go down."

When they landed on the bottom floor, they found Thomas Clarke inside the barn, hitching a horse to the wagon.

"How long have you two been in here?" Thomas had a look of shock in his eyes.

"From the beginning," Samuel answered.

"Samuel, surely thy parents are worried, this thou can'st be assured of."

"I'm afraid so, Mr. Clarke." Samuel responded.

"Come, I need thee," Thomas spoke as he grabbed a harness off the wall. "Harness the second mare to the cart," he said, pointing to the cart. "We'll pick up the wounded. Thou shalt help as well, Mary."

Samuel seemed relieved to have some work. For her part, Mary had to know about the silver epaulette on the ground. She ran from the barn, around to its back, and then down the hill toward William's fields. It took her only a few breathless moments to come upon the young captain. He lay on his stomach, his head turned toward the north. There was blood coming from a wound that she couldn't see. Next to him sat Peter, also wounded. He had his hand on the captain's shoulder, as if to comfort him.

"He's gone," Peter said with a strained voice. "Captain Shippen is gone."

"Oh," Mary whispered as she knelt down beside him.

"What am I to do?" Peter said. He looked lost, the tears creating paths through the dirt that caked his face. "He was a brother to me."

"I am sorry for thy loss, Peter, but thou art hurt, here." Mary touched his other arm, which hung loosely at his side. "Is there anyone who will help thee?" She looked around. She needed someone she could turn to, someone to tell her what to do with this wounded soldier. Coming toward them was an American soldier, checking the bodies that lay on the ground. Mary waved to him.

"You best get up to the house, son," he told Peter. "Can you help him?" he asked Mary.

"Yes." With the soldier's help, they were able to get Peter up to his feet. Mary could see his arm had been shattered and that a fragment of his bone stuck out from his flesh. She removed her apron and wrapped it around his arm. He winced in pain. Mary then helped Peter to walk up the hill to the house.

Sarah Clarke met Mary and Peter at the door. She was surprised to see Mary, but said nothing. Mary was too valued for the help she could lend to scold or send home.

"Take these," Sarah said, handing a bundle of rags to Mary. "And this," she continued with a bucket of water. "Clean what wounds thou can'st. Bind them enough to stop the bleeding."

"Yes," Mary said.

"Dr. Rush and the midwife will soon arrive. We must do what we can before they get here."

"It's General Mercer, make way, it's General Mercer," an American soldier called out to the individuals in the house. Gently and slowly, the men lifted up the general who had told Mary to stay in the barn. Sarah looked over his many wounds.

"In here," she said, pointing to the back bedroom off the kitchen.

"Where was he found?" Mary asked.

"Down the hill, by an oak tree."

More gunfire came from Nassau Hall in Princeton.

"They'll be taking the garrison now," the soldier who had brought Mercer in said. "We heard there were three hundred Americans held in the prison there. Is that so?"

"Yes," Sarah answered. "Mary, I think I see thy parents coming this way."

Mary drew in a sharp breath. She braced for a scolding, perhaps even a worse punishment for her outlandish conduct. She consoled herself that Samuel would get even worse for he was older, and should have kept her from harm's way.

"Mary!" Mrs. Stumpf said with relief.

"Miriam," Sarah grabbed hold of Mrs. Stumpf's arm, "we have need of thee, and Mary, too. Mary, tell thy mother thou hast regret, and then return to work."

"I am sorry, Mother, so sorry." Mary hung her head as she spoke. What a difficult child she had been to cause her parents so much worry over the last two days.

The entire day the mother and daughter attended to the wounded. In the afternoon, as the sun began its decline in the west, Mrs. Stumpf prepared a broth so that all could be fed. By that time, Cornwallis had arrived. When Cornwallis entered the Clarke House, he ordered his surgeon to care for all the wounded. War, Mary realized, had moments of peace, when soldiers cared for one another no matter what side they were on.

After the surgeon had attended to Peter's arm, Mary sat with him to spoon water into his mouth. To distract him from the immense pain he felt, she spoke to him.

"The captain, he was from where?"

"Philadelphia."

"And these green coats?"

"We are Continental Marines."

Mary helped Peter to lie down on a makeshift bed in the front room. Hannah Clarke handed her a bottle of brandy. Mary gently fed Peter the brandy until he fell asleep.

"Miss, miss," another male voice called out to Mary.

She turned to see a young soldier with a gash running from his lip to his temple. Taking a fresh rag, she dipped it in warm water and cleaned the long wound.

"Thanks to thee," he said.

She looked into his eyes, which were a brilliant green. "Thou art most welcome."

"Ah, another Friend."

"Yes, I am." Mary blushed and then looked away. She rinsed the rag she had used to clean his wound. "I can sew thee up."

"Will I be scarred, dost thou think?"

"Let's see." Mary examined the young man's gash carefully. "It's not that deep. What caused it?"

"A British bayonet."

"Oh."

"I was with General Mercer when he was ambushed. His horse was shot out from under him. The British soldiers surrounded him. I tried to help him but was bayoneted, and then hit, there," the young soldier turned his shoulder, "by the butt of a gun. I was stunned, helpless on the ground. One of the British soldiers said to General Mercer, 'Give quarter, you damn rebel general.' But the general said only "Nay, never.' He was bayoneted eleven times." He paused to take a deep breath. He then looked Mary straight in the eyes. "Ask me how I know."

"How dost thou know?"

"I counted each one, each thrust into his body."

The young man clenched his jaw down tightly. Mary dipped her rag and continued to clean the gash on his face. His green eyes were moist. Mary looked away. She would not dream of embarrassing him by watching his tears fall.

"I'll do it, miss," a surgeon's assistant, a young man about the same age as the wounded soldier, knelt down beside them.

From his kit, the surgeon's assistant pulled a needle and thread used to sew up wounds. As he stitched the young American's face, Mary stood.

"Would'st thou have some water to drink?" she asked the wounded one.

"Yes."

Mary went toward the kitchen. Before she walked up the step that led into it, she felt the young man's eyes on her. She stopped and turned to see him staring at her, without apology. She smiled, and then returned to her purpose of getting water. When she went back to him, his wound had been sewn shut.

Mary handed the cup of water to the young man. He couldn't smile, but in his eyes Mary could see his interest. Under regular circumstances, she would not grace him with her smile. However, these were not normal times. Here was a wounded American soldier who could not take his eyes from her. Inside, she felt confused by her situation. The battle, from this standpoint, was not so glorious. The idea these men fought for not only killed them. It caused them a great deal of suffering, it scarred them, it changed them forever.

Mary gave the young soldier her best smile before she turned away to help others.

Fourteen

Aftermath

It was a foggy morning when they came to take the bodies back to Philadelphia. General Mercer, laid neatly in his coffin, and Captain Shippen, first wrapped in linen shrouds provided by Mrs. Stumpf, were gently loaded onto the back of a wagon. Mary stood by the side of the road as the wagon, followed by a carriage that carried family members, passed by the farm. The captain, Mary sighed to admit it, had saved her and her brother. From others, Mary heard the story once more, how General Mercer had valiantly defied the British soldiers.

"Why? Why couldn't he surrender? He would be alive today if he had." Mary waited for Samuel to answer the question.

"Rumor has it that he, when he was young, was a surgeon's assistant at the Battle of Culloden."

"He was a surgeon?"

"Yes. He owns...that is he owned an apothecary in Virginia."

"But he's to be buried in Philadelphia."

"Because," Samuel continued, "he's from Scotland. Men from Scotland will bury him."

"Captain Shippen owned a grocery shop in Philadelphia."

"How dost thou know this?" Samuel asked.

"Peter told me." Mary sighed. "Peter is from Boston."

General Mercer and Captain Shippen became memories that Mary would never forget. How could she? Though General Washington and his army had left Princeton, they could never leave her mind. Those ten days when the Americans had saved their revolution were a part of Mary. A part of her family.

"Mr. Stockton is coming back to Princeton!" Paul announced at dinner that day. "He's been exchanged for British prisoners."

"This *is* an eventful day," Mrs. Stumpf said.

The rest of the day passed with chores and reading and nothing else. Life, it seemed, returned to some normalcy as soldiers passed out of Stony Brook and Princeton.

The next morning, Mr. Stumpf gently shook Mary awake.

"Have I overslept?"

"No."

Mary listened for the rooster to crow. He was silent.

"The sun is up. I have overslept."

"Just a little," Mr. Stumpf whispered. He paused as if to gather his thoughts. "Mary, this morning a wagon approaches Princeton."

"Yes?"

"I have received word, from Mr. Stockton, that Samuel and thee may want to meet this wagon. Mr. Stockton will be on it. He returns home."

Mary's heart began to beat faster.

"Why?" She swallowed hard. "Why would I want to see Mr. Stockton."

"Thy questions will be answered shortly. Dress, Mary, and I will take thee."

Mr. Stumpf left Mary's room. Only for the briefest time did she linger in her bed. After she had dressed by the kitchen fire, she opened the door to see Samuel waiting in the front room with their father.

In the yard, Paul stood with the cart. Samuel and Mary, each searching the other's face, sat in the back while Mr. Stumpf sat on the driver's bench. Paul handed his father the reins, and then stepped aside.

"Art thou warm, Mary? Samuel?" their father asked.

"Yes. Where do we go?"

"As I said, to Princeton."

Mr. Stumpf urged the horse forward.

"Dad?" Samuel asked.

Mr. Stumpf thought a moment before he responded. "Thou hast seen much these past few weeks, but this day concerns thy friend."

Samuel and Mary exchanged glances.

"Jimmy?" Mary said.

"Yes."

"What has happened?"

"He has been ill. Mr. Stockton is bringing him home. We are to meet the wagon to accompany Jimmy home."

"Is he wounded?" Mary asked.

"No. He is ill."

"Where was he?" Mary asked.

"Mr. Stockton was on a prison ship. So was Jimmy."

Mary felt crushed by the news. "I've heard tell of them, by the wounded after the battle at the Clarke Farm. These are awful places, empty, stripped down vessels, sitting in the cold of the water, without warmth, or beds. Men starve or die of diseases too awful."

"Be calm, Mary," Samuel said.

Mary looked across to her brother. He too had fear in his eyes. He looked away from her, his jaw tightening as he did so. She would, she told herself, have to stay in control of her emotions, even though the waiting seemed unbearable.

"Dad?"

"Yes Mary?"

"How sick is he?"

"I don't know."

The three turned to silence, each trying to assuage their own fear.

"Is that the wagon?" Samuel asked

Approaching from the opposite way was a large wagon. Mr. Stockton sat next to the driver.

"Yes."

Mr. Stumpf slowed the horse down. When the wagon drew nearer, he stopped the cart. He pulled the brake, jumped down, and then came around to help Mary descend to the road. Samuel hesitated. Slowly he rose to exit the cart. Mr. Stumpf took Mary's hand. Together, with Samuel somewhat behind, they walked toward Mr. Stockton who now stood next to the wagon. He was pale and thin.

"I'm sorry, Mary, Samuel, to have to tell you this, but Jimmy UpDyke died about an hour ago."

"No," Mary whispered.

Samuel looked straight ahead, his jaw firmly set. Mary ran around to the back of the wagon. There, under a blanket, was a body. She wanted to believe that it was all a mistake, that Jimmy couldn't be dead, that under that blanket was someone else. Her eyes traveled from the foot of the body to the head. There, peeking out from under the blanket were the unmistakable blond tresses that could belong only to Jimmy.

"Oh no," Mary gasped. She crawled up into the wagon and made her way to Jimmy's head. She pulled back the blanket to look into the face she so adored. "Jimmy, oh Jimmy," she said. She reached down to touch the face, marveling how sweet he looked in death.

Samuel jumped up into the wagon, his tears now freely flowing. "Jimmy, oh Jimmy, my friend."

"Let them ride with him to the UpDykes," Mr. Stockton said to Mr. Stumpf.

"I'll follow."

In her arms, Mary cradled Jimmy's head, placing it gently onto her lap. Samuel lay down beside him, his arm thrown over the dead friend's chest. From her place at the back of the wagon, Mary looked out to see her father watching his children.

When they reached the UpDykes, Mrs. UpDyke fainted away. Mr. UpDyke, the stoic one, thanked the Stumpf children for their friendship with his son. As Mary stepped back into the cart, Mr. Stockton held out a letter.

"He asked me to give this to thee."

Mary wanted to cry again, but instead, she stifled her tears. She reached out and took the letter. "I thank thee, Mr. Stockton."

"When was he taken prisoner?" Samuel asked, brushing away fresh tears.

"He was taken prisoner during the fall of Fort Washington. We met on a prison ship anchored on the Hudson. He was an amicable young man. I won't say he didn't suffer. He did. Yet he knew what he was about." Mr. Stockton paused. "He died for the sake of his country."

"He is so thin," Mary said.

"We were not well fed, and the dysentery was widespread."

"Thou hast suffered much, Mr. Stockton," Mary said.

Mr. Stockton smiled slightly, and then sighed. "I am alive. Now, I must get home to my family."

The next day, they buried Jimmy. Mr. Evans came, with his wife and children. During the service, Suzanna stared straight ahead. Mary barely noticed her. After the service, Mr. UpDyke approached Mary with a packet of letters in his hands.

"I hope you don't mind, Mary, but I had to read them." Mr. UpDyke held out to Mary all the letters she had written to him. "If you want to have them, you may. If not, his mother and I would treasure them."

"Keep them. I know them all, by heart."

That night, Mary curled up in the front room. One by one everyone went to bed, except for her. When she felt that everyone must be asleep, she pulled out the letter that Mr. Stockton had given her. By the light of the fire, she opened it. She noted that the letter had been written in haste.

To Mary Stumpf, James UpDyke sends greetings. I don't mean to alarm you Mary, but the British and Hessians are closing in on those of us who are trapped in Fort Washington. It is said by tomorrow we will be overrun. The captain says I will be taken prisoner, as I am only a drummer boy. For my part, I am sorry I'm not able to be of more service to my fellows in this army. General Washington has taken the bulk of the army across to the Jerseys. General Lee is somewhere in White Plains with the other half. There are only a few hundred of us here in the fort. Come what may, I hope to see you, perhaps in the summer. God bless you, James.

"Oh," Not wanting to wake her family she buried her head in the seat of the great chair while she cried.

All that night she did not sleep, for the crying would start and stop. Over the weeks that followed, she would cry without warning as soon as she thought of Jimmy. The idea of a life without him caused her unbearable pain. Mary thought she would never be happy again.

One day during the summer, her father found her crying as she pulled weeds in the kitchen garden. Mr. Stumpf took his daughter by the hand and led her down to the brook. There he gently splashed cold water on her face.

"'Tis no easy matter to lose someone we love."

Mary nodded her head.

"Time, Mary, will heal us, but we must give into life and the living of it. We cannot know why God calls us when He does, to return to Him. This is no matter to us for it's His decision, not ours."

"I mi-miss Jimmy so much."

"Mary, thou art alive. That too is not of thy doing, but God's will. Therefore, let thy wounds heal, and not fester. This is not to say that Jimmy shall leave thy heart. No, he is with thee, forever. But let him live in thy heart in happiness."

"How?"

"Be glad that thou wast important enough to him that he wrote to thee. His father tells me he wrote only to thee and his mother."

"To me, and his mother?"

"Yes."

Mary searched her father's face.

"What does this mean?"

"That he loved thee."

She grew silent. Then a slight smile curved her lips. "Why did I doubt him? Why?"

"Thou wast young and could not see what was before thee. But thou can'st see it now?"

"Yes. Yes."

Though sorrow would stay with her, what she now experienced was the sweetness of having a memory of a loved one. That he *had* loved her as she had loved him was all she needed to know. From that moment on, she no longer looked back. Only ahead.

Epilogue

Later that summer, Samuel, with his father's blessings, joined the army. Mrs. Stumpf and Mary feared for him, yet they learned to live with the uncertainty. One day, years later, when the war had ended, Samuel came home a young man of twenty-four. He stayed only for the briefest time, as he had met the sister of another man serving in the army. With this sister, Samuel had fallen in love.

In 1783, as the Congress met in Princeton, Samuel married his Priscilla, and they moved away to Pittsburg. Soon after, Paul married Rebecca and brought her to live on the Stumpf farm in a small house he built on the other side of the brook.

In the summer of 1784, Mary journeyed with Lazarus to Philadelphia, to stay with a sister of her mother's. There her younger cousin became the apprentice of a printer.

Mary loved the city. It was filled with the bustle of life. She visited the many shops that lined its busy streets. One day, as she crossed a street to get to a shop on the other side, Mary noticed a man walking toward her. Something about him seemed familiar. He too noticed her, and stared directly at her, studying her face intently. Mary should have felt uncomfortable. She didn't. Both kept walking, each toward the opposite side.

Mary's mind raced over memories as she tried to place the face. He was just past her when he stopped.

"Stony Brook," he said, firmly. "Thou art from Stony Brook."

Mary gasped. She stopped. How did he know? She turned back to face him.

He took a step forward. He was tall and able to look down directly into her face. He had brilliant green eyes. She still couldn't place him until she noticed the scar running from the corner of his mouth to his temple.

"Thou wast a soldier, wounded, on the Clarke farm."

"Yes." He smiled broadly.

"Get out of the road!" a man on a horse called out to them.

The young man took Mary's arm and led her to the other side. They stepped up on the walk.

"Thou art Mary. Mary Stumpf."

"How couldst thou recall that after all this time? Why, it's been seven years."

"A lifetime, Miss Stumpf."

Mary blushed. The walk was crowded with shoppers and others going about their business. The couple hampered the walkers' progress, forcing them to stop and go around.

"My name is Simon Wentworth."

"I am happy to meet thee." Mary could hardly look up at him as she had not felt such feelings since Jimmy.

"Again. Thou art happy to meet me *again*."

Mary gave a soft laugh, and he smiled broadly. He led Mary up the walk to a coffee house where they sat at a table by the window.

"Tell me all that has happened to thee, Miss Stumpf, since 1777."

"What? Oh, thou art a humorous man."

"I am a serious man. I have passed the examination and have entered the profession of apothecary. I will one day take over my father's business. In short, Miss Stumpf, my prospects in life are excellent."

"I see."

"May I call on thee? By the by, dost thou now live in Philadelphia?"

"I visit an aunt."

"Come," he said, standing and holding out his arm to her. "I ask to meet her to present myself to her. I have to know."

"Have to know what?"

"What thine aunt will say."

Mary blushed again. She looked away from Simon as she took his arm.

At her aunt's home, the three of them had tea. From their conversation, Mary learned that the Wentworth family had come to Philadelphia from Britain when Simon was only three years of age. After Simon left, Mary anxiously awaited her aunt's opinion of the young man who had so suddenly come a courting Mary.

"The Wentworths are good people, Mary. The question is, what think'st thou of him?" her aunt said. "What dost thou feel for Simon? Give thyself time to think on it."

Mary went to the garden to sit under the guardianship of the large tree in its center. She leaned against the trunk, closing her eyes to the present, allowing the distant memories to flood into her mind's eye. Those things that she would never forget had been a part of what had formed her. Some would say that her adventures with the War for

Independence should be forgotten. Mary would disagree. Those memories, of the battles, of the deaths of the Hessian and of Jimmy, were sad.

Yet she had witnessed the birth of her nation, in spite of the violence and depressed moments, and she had seen the success of the enterprise. The soldiers in the fields had brought that enterprise to success, assisted by the women who stayed on farms, or traveled with their soldier husbands. The men of Congress, too, had ensured the revolution, with the help of wives who counseled them. All had acted on a wide stage not only for themselves. They acted for her and others like her, the next generation. Jimmy had died so that she could sit under this tree in peace as a citizen of her own nation. She honored him by living a full life.

Mary sighed. "They are bittersweet those memories I have. Yet now, at this moment here, they are more sweet than bitter."

Mary smiled. She recalled the excitement she had felt at the Battle of Princeton, not only during the fighting, but afterward, when that young wounded soldier stared so intently at her. If she had not taken the chance to be a witness to the events of January 3, 1777, she would not have opened the door to come face to face with her future. This, then, was the joy of not holding back on life. A life fully lived today gives way to a tomorrow without limits.

What did Mary think of Simon Wentworth? She married him.

More Mary Stories are coming. Next up, in 2014

Mary de Cotten
At the signing of the Magna Carta

Mary de Cotten is the daughter of a Norman father and a Saxon mother. She lives in thirteenth century England. Join her as she finds herself caught up in the rebellion of the Barons in 1215. She risks her life for the fight for basic human rights during the reign of King John.

www.ingramcontent.com/pod-product-compliance
Lightning Source LLC
Chambersburg PA
CBHW072000170626
46813CB00005B/1942